AMBUSH

OTHER BOOKS BY OBERT SKYE

THE PILLAGY SERIES
Pillage
Choke

THE WORLD OF FOO
Leven Thumps and the Gateway to Foo
Leven Thumps and the Whispered Secret
Leven Thumps and the Eyes of the Want
Leven Thumps and the Wrath of Ezra
Leven Thumps and the Ruins of Alder
Professor Winsnicker's Book of Proper Etiquette
    for Well-Mannered Sycophants
Beyond Foo, Book 1: Geth and the Return of the Lithens

THE CREATURE FROM MY CLOSET SERIES
Book 1: Wonkenstein

AMBUSH

OBERT SKYE

SHADOW
MOUNTAIN

FOR KRISTA

WORDS MAY FAIL ME, BUT YOU NEVER DO

Visit us at ShadowMountain.com

Library of Congress Cataloging-in-Publication Data
Skye, Obert, author.
    Ambush / Obert Skye.
        pages cm.
    Sequel to: Choke.
    Summary: Beck, Kate, and Wyatt thought they had finished hatching dragons from stones but when they are proved wrong, Beck must decide if acting on the inherited Pillage family traits will gain him what he really wants.
    ISBN 978-1-60908-891-0 (hardbound : alk. paper)
    1. Magic—Fiction.   2. Dragons—Fiction.   3. Blessing and cursing—Fiction.   4. Eccentrics and eccentricities—Fiction.   5. Young adult fiction, American. [1. Dragons—Fiction.   2. Magic—Fiction.   3. Blessing and cursing—Fiction.   4. Eccentrics and eccentricities—Fiction.   5. Uncles—Fiction.]   I. Title.
    PZ7.S62877Amb 2012
    [Fic]—dc23   2011032672

Printed in the United States of America
R. R. Donnelley, Crawfordsville, IN

10   9   8   7   6   5   4   3   2   1

Contents

Sure, it might not have been the wisest thing to say, but it was honest. I had said my piece, now it was time to just sit still and appear remorseful.

My father, Aeron, looked at me and closed his eyes. He opened them back up, and his head bobbled slightly. I could almost feel the tongue-lashing I was about to receive. I held my hand up in front of my face, preparing for the sharp words that were about to rain down.

"Beck, you must plant that stone," he whispered fearlessly.

I put my hand down and looked around.

"What?" I asked, not believing for a moment what I was hearing. It was no tongue-lashing, but it was almost equally frightening.

"The stone," he said urgently. "You must plant it."

"I can't..."

"You don't understand," he interrupted. "You must. None of this will change until that last stone is planted and this is finished."

I'll be honest; I had not seen the conversation going this way. And in that same spirit of honesty, I'll admit I wasn't disappointed about it.

"Plant that stone," he said.

I was nothing if not obedient.

CHAPTER 1

It's All Too Much

THE MOOD INSIDE THE ROOM WAS HEAVY. Kate held the stone in her hands as if it were a baby made of brittle glass. Streaks of new moon slipped through the windows of the manor and painted the room in shades of gray and shadow. The rock she held shimmered lightly, and Kate appeared prettier than I was willing to admit. Her red hair hung forward and down over the stone as she gazed at it with her deep blue eyes.

"This is the last one?" she asked.

"The very last," I replied.

Wyatt stood next to me, breathing slowly. His dark hair and stout build made him look tougher than I knew he was. Wyatt had been one of my worst enemies when I had arrived in Kingsplot. Now, however, we were friends. He was still annoying at times, but I liked him. Kate, Wyatt, and I had been through plenty in the last little while and now there was just one more thing we needed to take care of before I could breathe easier.

"Are you sure we shouldn't keep it?" Wyatt asked, his green eyes wide. "We can just lock it up. I mean what harm can it cause locked up in my room?"

"Are you nuts?" Kate whispered. "You've seen what the other stones have grown. Who knows what kind of dragon this last one holds?"

I stared at the six-inch-long, oval-shaped, marbled stone. It was gray with ribbons of white and gold running through it. I sighed, knowing that if I wanted I could take it, plant it, and bring something otherworldly to life—something I could use to pillage and stake claim to the spoils my ancestors had gotten rich on. Of course, the last dragon I had grown had almost killed me and Kate. And the ones before that had torn apart the town of Kingsplot. Still, despite the danger dragons were capable of producing, the thought of holding onto the stone was tempting.

"Don't even think about it," Kate insisted. "You have to get rid of it."

"I know," I said defensively. "Besides, I'm tired of getting beat up by every bush and plant around here."

My family had some sort of weird control over things that grew. Plants and vegetation seemed to respond and grow for us in ways that they normally didn't do. I could make leaves float and trees move, and, of course, with the right stones I could even grow dragons. But lately Mother Nature was beating the life out of me. Every tree I passed pinched me. Bushes reached out to trip me. The lawns in front of the manor had found ways of bubbling up and knocking me to the ground where they would give me wicked grass burns. I was convinced that the only way for the beatings to stop was to let go of this last stone.

We tried to break the rock up with a hammer, but no luck. We then dropped it off the side of a huge cliff, but it still didn't break. It was proving to be indestructible. We considered mailing it somewhere far off, but we couldn't be sure where it would ultimately end up. Wyatt wanted to pitch it into a lake or river, but I knew that in time it would wash up into the wrong hands.

So, we had turned to the manor for the solution.

The Pillage manor was a seven-story stone wonder. It was not only my home, but it was a place of great mystery and many secrets. There were passages behind walls, and tunnels under its foundation. Mysterious doors were walled up, and bits of the floor had compartments and stairs quietly tucked beneath them. I had found dumbwaiters that seemed to go nowhere and cabinets and holes that were all wallpapered or bricked over.

I loved the manor.

Two weeks ago I had found a dusty, dark chute in one of

the unused utility rooms on the bottom floor. I had been exploring the manor and noticed it hidden in a dark corner behind piles of old junk. It was just one more find in the line of cool things the manor was hiding.

Wyatt and I had dropped a few things down it and could hear no bottom. We had thrown sticks down and even lowered an old rope, but we still couldn't feel or sense any end to the hole. There was also no sign of it on the floor below, and the part of the basement it would have gone through was still packed with dirt. What it really was, was a mystery, but I figured it would be the perfect place to drop the stone. I knew it would be next to impossible to reach it again once it had been released. I also liked the idea that I would still know where it was. I wouldn't have to worry about it being found by someone else, and it was only fitting that the manor would be its gravestone.

Kate handed me the rock. It glowed like a weak light bulb in my hands.

"Maybe that stone grows a *good* dragon," Wyatt said, making one last attempt to stop me from getting rid of it.

"I don't think so," Kate said sadly.

I pulled open the chute door and looked down into the dark hole.

"I'm not sure I want to do this," I whispered softly.

"You have to," Kate whispered back.

Since moving to Kingsplot I had changed drastically. The old me would have never gone along with something just because it was the right thing to do. But I knew I had to do this because lately life was just too much and it felt as if putting this stone to rest would help things calm down.

"What if there's an animal or something down there?" I asked ridiculously.

"There's no animal down there," Kate said kindly. "Drop the rock."

Wyatt looked away. I reached out and tried to drop the rock. I guess my palms were kind of sweaty because it wouldn't leave my hands. I pulled it back in and put it on the ground. After wiping my hands dry on my shirt, I picked the stone up again. I was wondering if the stone would allow me to drop it, or if it would come up with some other way so that I wouldn't let it go.

Wyatt leaned in closer to see what the holdup was. He bumped me, and the stone bobbled in my hands for a few seconds and then—as we watched in slow motion—it fell to the ground and rolled to the rim of the chute. It hung there for a second or two and then . . . dropped over the edge. Someone yelped; it might have been me. We could hear it scrape and bang the sides of the metal chute as it descended far below. The fading sound continued for some time before it grew too faint to hear any longer. All three of us just stood there in silence, staring at the open mouth of the dark chute. I think we were all waiting for the chute to belch the stone back up. After a few minutes of nothing, I sighed.

"I feel awful," I admitted.

Kate put her arm around me. Her red hair brushed up against my right ear, and I could hear her breathing softly. She smelled like something much more becoming than a musty old manor.

"I'm impressed," she said kindly. "You got rid of it."

I wasn't going to quibble about the technicalities that it sort of dropped in the chute without my help. My mind raced as I tried to think of another time when Kate had actually been impressed with me. I mean I knew she liked me, but impressed?

"Really?" I asked. "You're impressed?"

"Slightly," she said while kissing me on the cheek. "I know that wasn't easy."

"Come on," Wyatt complained. "Do you two mind knocking that off until I'm not around?"

I closed the top of the chute and snapped the latch. The three of us then left the room slowly, foolishly thinking that we would never have to worry about stones or dragons again.

CHAPTER 2

I've Just Seen a Face

HEAVING AND COUGHING, the yellow bus inched along the cobblestone road like a caterpillar with stiff joints and a rumbling belly. It swerved to avoid an old man walking an even older dog along the side of the road. All of us swayed to the right and then swayed back into place, jiggling like springs. A few students complained about being jostled, but not me, it was the first exciting thing that had happened all day. I looked at Kate as she sat next to me on the bus seat.

"We're almost there," she said as if I needed to hear it.

"Great," I replied. "I'm trying not to be too excited."

Kate ignored my perfectly good sarcasm and turned to gaze out one of the side windows. Through the windshield I could see the two other school buses moving in front of us. Like ours, they were filled with students who were all on their way to a museum.

"Look on the bright side, Beck," Kate replied. "It's nice to be out of our school and enjoying the weather."

Kate had ignored my sarcasm, so now I ignored hers. The weather in Kingsplot today was like the weather yesterday, and most likely the weather tomorrow—misty, with a chance of more mist and prolonged gloom. The sun was up there some-where, but it was anyone's guess when it might actually man up and step out from behind the clouds to show itself.

"Did you bring a camera?" Kate asked.

"Why would I need a camera?" I asked honestly. "It's a mu-seum. I'm pretty sure seeing everything once will be plenty. It's a field trip, not a memorable event."

The field trip I was talking about had been a surprise to all of us. Last week Professor Squall had told our class that if we all caught up on our work we would be rewarded. So the entire class had worked as hard as we could. Then yesterday he informed us that the reward was a field trip to the town mu-seum—and most of our class felt ripped off. True, a few of the kids tried to act excited, but they all had a reputation for being kiss-ups.

"I was hoping the reward involved food," I said. "Or early release from school, or maybe a new car."

"You get to ride on a bus next to me," Kate said, smiling.

I told her she needed to work on being more humble.

I don't know why I was bothered about the field trip. It's not like I would prefer to be sitting in my classroom. Besides I had positive things to think about. There was only one more month until summer break, I was getting straight B's, I had turned seventeen a couple of weeks earlier, and I hadn't done anything to mess up too badly since the last time I had messed up.

"Remember the dragons?" I whispered to Kate, thinking back to one of my many messes.

"Of course," she whispered back.

I looked at the other students on the bus and wondered why nobody ever mentioned the pillage now. The town of Kingsplot was weird. It seemed that there was something about the air that made people's minds foggy. It amazed me that people didn't discuss daily the pillaging that had taken place well over a year ago. The magic and misty air of the Hagen Valley seemed to be wiping most people's brains clean. Occasionally someone would point at me and say, "You." But that was the worst of it anymore. No reporters came around, and the outside world either had lost interest and written it off as a hoax, or didn't acknowledge it, or had forgotten.

At the moment the town of Kingsplot was almost completely put back together. Buildings that had been damaged once again looked like their old stodgy selves. Roses grew on brick walls and along the cobblestone streets, looking like they always had. Any new construction already seemed to look old and weathered and as nonglamorous as any place could appear. People went about their business as if there were no reason to stop and marvel at what had once happened in their simple lives, as if their minds were determined to forget the past and move slowly and quaintly into the future.

"Look at that cloud," Kate said, pointing out the side window. "It looks like Lizzy."

The Lizzy Kate was referring to was the dragon we had most recently raised. The long white cloud did look like Lizzy with her wings spread out and her long tail whipping behind her. The head wasn't exactly right, but I could clearly see the resemblance. The real Lizzy had been majestic and intoxicating. Her presence had drawn us in like a strong magnet. Her skin was opalescent and shimmered like the edge of a strong dream. We had fallen in love with her, but in the end she changed and attempted to kill everyone I loved. It had taken everything we had to stop her. It had been just over two months now since Lizzy had died. The parts of the Pillage manor and garage that had been damaged were put back together, and life was carrying on in the slow, wet fashion of everyday Kingsplot.

The yellow school bus pulled to a stop right behind the

two other buses and next to the curb directly in front of the museum. The street we were on was sloped so as I stood up, I, along with everyone else, stumbled forward and out the front door. As a good friend, I shoved Wyatt out the exit.

It wasn't raining today, and the clouds were just high enough that we could see for a few miles. I stood there with Wyatt, looking around. The Kingsplot museum was called Wiggendale, named after one of the important people who had lived here years ago, Cedric Wiggendale. It was a large, brown brick building shaped like a fat rectangle. It had hundreds of square, opaque front windows and a crown of slate gray stone that ran along the length of the top. The Wiggendale Museum was located next to Lake Mend, the largest lake in the Hagen Valley.

The spot where Wiggendale sat was often referred to as the loveliest spot in town—at least that's what the big wooden sign near the lakeshore claimed. There were roses everywhere and rolling green lawns that seemed to spill over the edges and into the water. This morning, however, the beauty was muted, and the scene looked washed-out and lifeless.

The Wiggendale building itself was interesting, but it really wasn't any more impressive than the huge stone manor I lived in. In fact, part of the reason it was hard for me to get hyped about this field trip was because I felt like I already lived in a museum.

Ever since I had moved to Kingsplot I had been surrounded by old things—an old father, an old house, old grounds, an old school, and old problems that my ancestors had cooked up years ago.

"I'm already bored," Wyatt said as we all walked toward the building.

The brick walkway leading to the front of the museum was wet from mist, and at least three students slipped and fell down as we walked into the building. None of them got hurt, but it made me wish I had brought a camera. While walking to the front door, I thought I heard a couple of the rosebushes growl at me.

"Did you hear that?" I asked Kate, pointing at one of the bushes.

"Hear what?" she replied.

I looked at the silent rosebushes. Ever since we had dropped the final stone down the hidden chute in the manor, nothing treelike nor growing had bothered me. It was so nice to walk confidently through the woods without worrying that some fern would strangle me.

"I think that bush growled," I explained.

"Come on," Kate said, smiling. "That doesn't happen anymore."

Right inside the front door of Wiggendale was a big mural of Kingsplot, painted years ago by a man who supposedly had no arms. Next to the mural was an old photo of the actual artist painting with his feet. I was pretty impressed.

Just past the mural was a large display of cactuses in a fake Southwest setting. The scene was supposed to represent the landscape that early pioneers had left to come East and settle the Hagen Valley. Next to that was a room filled with flags and old license plates nailed to the wall.

I didn't wonder for a second why I didn't come here more often. Everywhere I looked I could see ancient, dusty artifacts. To my left was an old bike that the first mayor of Kingsplot had once ridden. To my right was a huge picture of Kingsplot fifty years ago, which looked almost the same as it did today. And directly in front of me was a really old security guard with a huge gray mustache. He was wearing a uniform and had a billy club strapped to his waist. His wide brown eyes looked frightened by all the students now pouring in through the front doors. He backed up a few steps and tried to blend into the wall.

I had never felt safer.

I heard our teacher Professor Squall across the room loudly telling someone to not touch something.

"Maybe that's the problem," I whispered to Kate.

"What problem?" she asked.

"With museums," I clarified. "You can't touch anything here. Who knows if all this junk is even real?"

Kate pointed toward a suitcase that was sitting on a table.

There was a sign underneath it that read: Duke Elliott's official travel luggage.

"Are you saying that's not real?" Kate asked.

"Who knows?" I replied. "It could just be a hologram." I reached out and touched the suitcase—it wasn't a hologram. As I was pulling my hand back, a man to my right shouted.

"Don't touch!"

The man who was using his outdoor voice indoors was the museum director. I knew this because he had on a badge that read: Museum Director. Mr. Museum smiled the sort of smile that suggested he was on to me and then cleared his throat and turned to look at all the students. He was a slight man with tiny hands and large, perfectly round nostrils that twitched and expanded as he breathed. He had droopy ears and a Band-Aid on his forehead. Above the Band-Aid was a head of very thick black hair.

"Good day, students," he said seriously, his thick, sticky voice as unusual as his appearance. "Today I desire for you all to see things which will provoke the sedentary mind and open your eyes to hissssssssstory."

We all stared respectfully at him.

"History," he clarified, as if the drawn-out hissy version was too much for our sedentary minds to understand.

A few of us nodded to let him know that we understood and that he could move on. He slowly led us from room to room talking about pictures and dusty objects that probably should have been thrown out years ago. He pointed to what looked like an old jug and said, "The winds of change can often blow with calmness and grace."

I leaned over and whispered into Kate's right ear. "What's that have to do with that jug?"

"I have no idea," she whispered back.

"We have way older stuff in my house," I reminded her.

"Right," Kate replied softly. "But that junk's not important to Kingsplot."

"Actually, I bet it's more important than this stuff," I argued. "Kingsplot wouldn't be what it is if it hadn't been for my family and their junk."

"Excuse me?" the tiny hand man said, apparently bothered by the fact that Kate and I were talking while he was. "Is there a tidbit of information you wish to share with the whole of us?"

I couldn't really understand his phraseology, but I knew from his inflection that he was asking a question.

"Well?" he asked impatiently. "What do you have to say?"

I thought about continuing to ignore him, but being the polite young man that I was, I tossed out an answer.

"Museums?"

The museum curator stared at me as if I were an exhibit he wished had been discontinued. He looked at Professor Squall and shook his head. Professor Squall sighed loudly and then walked over and stood next to Kate and me.

"Beck, we don't need any extra commentary from you today," Squall insisted in a whisper. "This man is very important and has graciously volunteered to give us a bit of his time."

"Sorry," I said, trying to sound sincere without too many extra words.

Mr. Museum cleared his throat and continued talking. He went on about an old tattered flag, waving his miniature marshmallow fingers around. After he gushed about the flag, he went on and on about a big clay pole for a few minutes. I had no idea there was so much to be said about a clay pole, but he was filled to the top of his furry head with info. After the pole talk, he led us as a group into a different room.

The new room was large—the ceilings were twenty feet high—and painted gray. The walls were dirty, and I could see dark mold along the baseboards. I thought about pointing that out and demanding that I be allowed to leave and breathe fresh air, but I knew Squall wouldn't go for it. In the middle of the room was a gigantic clear ball that was filled with half-inch metal balls. The massive orb looked like the top of a huge gumball machine with shiny steel gumballs inside. It was six feet tall, and I could see dust on the very top of it. Surrounding the sphere were a dozen or so life-sized iron statues of women and men. A low, red velvet rope circled the entire display to keep people from getting too close.

Mr. Museum—or Mr. M as I now affectionately called him in my mind—stopped in front of the large sphere and asked, "Do you know what we have here?"

One of the super-genius girls from the other class raised her hand. Mr. M pointed toward her like he was pressing an invisible doorbell.

"Those are steel ball bearings in there," the girl informed us all. "They were made at the old steel mill on the other side of Lake Mend."

"Good answer," the curator said. "You are a friend of history."

"And," the girl continued, "that mill has been closed for years, but it was the main employer in Kingsplot for a very long time."

"Fantastic," Mr. M said. "And the container of ball bearings is surrounded by the statues of the men and women who built and ran the factory. They in turn helped build up the town of Kingsplot here in the Hagen Valley. All of us owe them a great debt of gratitude for what we now enjoy."

I looked around, wondering exactly what we were enjoying.

Mr. M praised Smart Girl some more and then pointed across the room toward an old car. He waved his tiny hands to motion for us to move away from the orb. Everyone except me followed like sheep addicted to history. I had seen old cars before, but I'd never seen so many shiny metal balls in one container, and something inside of me wanted to touch the display. I leaned over the red velvet rope and put my right hand against the plastic sphere. It was cold. The plastic felt like a window in autumn, and a small chill ran up my arms and caused my body to shiver slightly. I stared at all the silver ball bearings inside. The millions of shiny balls were transfixing.

Kate had walked off with the group, but she turned around and saw me touching the round display. She made some sort of hissing noise while shaking her head. I took my hands off the huge sphere and leaned back out over the rope. I stood tall and tried to make it look like I was paying attention. Kate rolled her blue eyes and turned away. Mr. M was saying something about how the car he was pointing at once belonged to the third mayor of Kingsplot. He then paused. I clapped because I thought I should. Everyone turned to look at me.

"Excuse me?" Mr. M asked.

"Nothing," I said, my face turning slightly red. "I was just clapping about the car."

Mr. M made an expression that looked similar to one a person might make if they had accidentally stepped in cat vomit with their bare feet.

"Sorry," I tried.

He sniffed in a passive-aggressive way and then went back to talking about the old car. Everyone turned away from me as they continued to listen to him. I looked at Kate for support. Her expression looked similar to the one a person might make if they suddenly realized they were dating an idiot. She turned away and gave all her attention to the speaker.

Hanging my head, I sighed. I looked at the large plastic ball with the ball bearings. The millions of silver balls were spellbinding. I could see shapes and shadows all throughout the globe. I looked over at Mr. M and tried to act interested.

He was now telling everyone about how the mayor's car had a secret compartment in it. Normally that was something I would care about, but at the moment I had millions of silver balls on my mind. Plus, the statues surrounding it were cool looking. The still metal faces and expressions of those who had once lived here were hypnotizing. One of the statues behind the plastic orb even looked oddly familiar. I wanted to step over the rope and take a better look, but I forced my feet to keep still. I needed Mr. M and the crowd of students to move on. There was something about that statue's face that I needed to examine.

CHAPTER 3

Help

ALL I COULD DO WAS WAIT. It took all the patience I could muster not to move instantly. But just as soon as everyone had walked to the other side of the room and was fully distracted by the new displays Mr. M was squawking about, I quietly stepped over the low velvet rope and moved closer to the display.

I walked carefully between a bronze statue of a woman named Emily Welt and a short bronze statue of a man labeled Dan Gardiner, who was wearing a hat. Next to the plastic ball was a tall bronze statue of a guy with a short beard and puffy sleeves. I stared at his face, half expecting him to say something to me.

He didn't.

I looked down toward his feet and read the metal plaque near his shins.

"Pillage," I whispered in surprise.

I bent down and looked at the dusty plaque. There was no first name or any other marking, just the single word, *Pillage*. I straightened up and looked directly into the statue's cold metal eyes. I had no idea exactly who he was or what he had to do with the ball bearing factory. I supposed if I were forced to guess, I would have guessed that he was my great-grandfather Taft. Of course, it could also not be my great-grandfather, or he could be another Pillage altogether.

Mr. M, Kate, and all of the students moved out of the room, leaving me completely alone. I touched my bronze relative on the right shoulder. I was probably just being dramatic, but I swear I felt a small shock run through my arm and charge the back of my neck with goose bumps. Suddenly this museum didn't seem so dumb. The statue represented my family, and I wanted family. I know at my age a lot of kids push away from their families, but I felt differently. I wanted my father to get out of the hospital and for him to be all right. I wanted the sickness and confusion that swirled through so many of my ancestors' brains to be gone forever.

"I wish you could talk," I said quietly to the statue.

There was no reply from the statue, but I could hear a soft crackling, like the sound of static, growing around me. I listened carefully in an attempt to decipher where it was coming from.

"Beck?" Kate's voice called softly, surprising me and cutting through the sound of the soft static.

I jumped an inch.

"Beck, are you still in here?" she whispered loudly.

I smiled because Kate had come back for me.

"Here," I called out to her.

Kate looked at me as I stood on the other side of the velvet rope among the statues.

"What are you doing?" she asked.

"Come here," I said with excitement.

"No," she said responsibly. "We need to get back to the group."

"Just for a second," I insisted. "Come look at this."

Kate looked around. She glanced into the other room where everyone was and pushed her long red hair back behind her right ear.

"Really quick," I promised.

Kate was one of the most independent and intelligent girls I knew. Yet for some reason she listened to me. She stepped over the low velvet rope and weaved between the statues to where I was.

"Look," I said, pointing down.

Kate looked at the plaque and shrugged. "Who is it, one of your crazy relatives?"

"I think so."

"Which one is . . . ?" Kate stopped talking. "Wait, do you hear that?" she asked.

The faint cackle of static was growing louder once more—like a radio being slowly turned up.

"I don't know what that is," I whispered. "The sound system must have a broken speaker or something."

"I don't think that's the sound system," Kate gasped, pointing down and toward the wall closest to the display.

I looked down and jumped back just a bit. The floor looked like it was bubbling around the edges of the room. I glanced around and could see huge brown mounds bubbling up from the baseboards.

"Are those . . . ?"

"Mushrooms!" Kate exclaimed.

Mushroom caps the size of cantaloupes were pushing up from the mold below the baseboards and sending out long shoots that sliced through the air like wet spaghetti noodles. The entire edge of the room looked like it was boiling with dirty brown water. Mushrooms sprang from every crack and corner, wherever tiny bits of mold gave them life.

"Are you doing that?" Kate cried, backing up into my arms.

"I'm not doing anything!" And I put my arms around her to prove it.

Once again, the vegetation was after me. I stared at the fungi growing out of the mold. It was gargantuan and cancerous looking. The mushroom caps began to pop free from their stems and roll toward us. They were bouncing off the displays like fleshy bubbles.

One of us screamed.

"That's not going to help!" Kate yelled back.

I held onto Kate tightly as the mushrooms bounced toward us from all directions. One mushroom cap the size of a fat tomato slapped me in the face as strands of fungi wrapped around our legs. We both decided that now was the perfect moment to scream for help. We opened our mouths, but before anything came out, Professor Squall came walking in from the other room calling my name. Apparently he had noticed that his most troublesome student was no longer with the group, and he had come to round me up.

"Beck!" he barked. "Beck!"

Instantly, every mushroom in motion dropped to the ground.

"Beck, are you in here?" Professor Squall hollered.

Kate and I stood still between the statues and the ball bearing-filled orb. We had been about to call for help, but now that help was here and the mushrooms were still, I wasn't so sure I wanted to be saved.

"Beck, is that you?" Squall asked loudly. He moved in our direction and stepped on a big, meaty mushroom that was stretched out from the baseboard and reaching in mine and Kate's direction. He looked down.

"What in the . . . ?" Professor Squall glanced around at the large, fleshy clumps of mushrooms lying all over the ground and sticking to the walls.

I could see a thick, dark shade of red rising from beneath his shirt collar and spreading up over his face.

"Beck!"

Kate pushed out of my arms and moved behind the Pillage bronze statue to hide. I think I was going to turn and run, but as I swiveled, my right foot slipped on a wad of mushroom and I went careening into my metal relative. The impact caused the statue to skid off its base and tip toward the ball bearing-filled sphere. I grabbed the right arm of the statue to try and pull it back, but the balance was all off and the weight of it was too great to pull it back. I dug my heels into the ground in an effort to push back and keep the statue from falling farther. Sweat dripped from my forehead and into my eyes. I looked toward Kate as she continued to selfishly try and hide.

"Beck!" Squall yelled. "What are you doing?"

Kate glanced at me. Her blue eyes were as wide as donuts, and her jaw had dropped so low I could clearly see that she had no cavities. I stared at her and mouthed, "Help."

The statue slipped farther. Clearly there was nothing Kate could do to help me, so she silently mouthed a couple of words of her own.

"We're dead."

The statue was too heavy. It slipped farther off the base, and my sweaty fingers lost their grip. The figure seemed to tip in slow motion toward the plastic orb. The right shoulder of the statue hit the ball bearing-filled ball and knocked the whole thing two inches off its base.

I could see and hear all the silver balls in the massive globe shifting.

"Beck, stop that this instant!" Squall yelled.

The students in the other room had come back through the archway to see what all the shouting was about. Their eyes rested on me as I stood there next to the fallen statue.

I was now sweating like mad, but I smiled one of my smiles that I knew old people appreciated, but that everyone else found suspicious. Everyone just looked at me; then, as if all of their necks were on the same hinge, they simultaneously looked toward the still-settling orb as it rocked on the side of its base. Things were about to go from bad to worse.

"Grab that scoundrel!" Mr. M yelled.

The ball bearings within the plastic orb shifted more, causing the entire thing to drop from its stand and onto the floor. Everyone screamed as the four-foot plastic sphere began to roll slowly toward them. I tried to push back against it and force it to stop, but it was so heavy it knocked me onto my rear. I banged up against the floor with a thud. I would have sat up and looked for sympathy from my fellow students, but they all had problems of their own. The ball was gaining momentum.

Everyone began to scatter out of the ball's path. I knew what I had just done was wrong, but it was pretty magical watching that massive orb roll across the floor heading directly toward all the other students. It wasn't rolling really fast, but as the ball bearings inside shifted and tumbled, it made the most spectacular noise. It knocked over two other displays and was leaving a trail of greasy, smeared mushrooms behind. Most students had their hands above their heads bouncing against each other in an all-out panic. The sphere rolled past the car display and bumped up against the east wall. It hit the wall hard, but the plastic display somehow stayed intact and stopped.

Everyone froze. We all just stood there staring at the sphere. The room was now incredibly silent. I could hear my heaving heart and my heavy breathing. All at once everyone seemed to remember me. They turned their heads and looked back to where I was now standing.

I opened my mouth to calmly explain myself, but once again the huge orb stole my thunder. It shot out an eardrum-shattering crack. It creaked violently and then with a tremendous pop, it just split in half. Millions of ball bearings flowed out like metallic water flooding a dry room.

The shouts of students combined with the sound of all those silver balls rolling over the floor and pinging up against each other was deafening. I could see people falling to the ground as they slipped and tripped over the metal marbles. Mr. M ran in place for a few seconds and then slammed to the ground. Wyatt was sliding on his back across the floor. Kate stayed put behind her statue.

I thought about sticking around, but something inside me wanted out. My body turned, and I ran for the front door. Like so many moments of my life, I had no idea what I was doing; all I knew was that I needed to split.

Ball bearings swirled around my feet as I ran. My right foot slipped out and I flew toward the front door, sliding on my chest. I picked myself up as quickly as I could and ran through the cactus room and out the front door. I stumbled, and the doors slammed behind me. The screams of everyone inside were now muffled and faint. There was nobody in front of the

Wiggendale Museum but me. I could see the three empty buses at the curb, and I ran to the one at the back.

I pushed open the front door and climbed inside.

I ran down the aisle and sat on the backseat, ducking down to hide. My breathing was erratic and loud. I looked out the windows toward the front door of the museum. Nobody had followed my lead and come out yet. I put my head in my hands and tried to think of a way out of this disaster.

"Why?" I moaned, wondering why I was so good at making a mess of things. My life had finally begun to settle down a bit, and now I had gone and done this.

I saw the front doors of the museum burst open. Mr. M and Professor Squall came charging out with the students behind them. Someone pointed in the direction of the buses as another student yelled my name and pointed directly toward me.

I was in big trouble. My mind started to make up possible excuses. "I was trying to free the captive ball bearings." "I got so excited about history I wanted to bring it to life." "I thought the permission slip I had signed gave me permission to cause trouble." "I'm an idiot." The last one definitely sounded the most believable.

Mr. M and Professor Squall started running toward the bus I was on. I ducked down between the seats, but I knew I had been spotted. Everyone was screaming and, like an angry mob with backpacks and notebooks, they stormed closer. I looked to the front of the bus where the door was still open. It didn't make a ton of sense, but I thought that if I could close the door and keep them out, I would at least be safe for the moment.

I ran down the aisle to the front of the bus as the sea of students swarmed closer. I was sweating even more. My hands were wet, and my shirt was sticking to my back. A few of the faster students were now just a couple of feet away from the open door. I leaped over the driver's seat and crashed down against the steering wheel. I was dazed, but I had enough wits about me to grab the door lever and pull it as hard as I could. The door slammed shut just moments before the first assailants arrived. Two boys I recognized but didn't really know began to pound on the door, ordering me to open up.

"I don't know how!" I yelled back, trying to act like I had no clue how to open the door.

"We just saw you close it!" one of them yelled.

I twisted in the driver's seat and pulled hard on the door lever. I didn't want there to be any chance of the door coming open. I kicked my feet against the floor and pushed up to get more leverage and keep my grip on the handle. There were dozens of students now banging on the door and side of the bus. Their hollering intensified as their pounding began to get even more frantic. It sounded like I was inside some giant tribal drum. I thought I heard someone yell, "You're grooving!"

I was confused for a moment, but then I looked out. I saw the trees slowly move past the door. My heart grew to the size of a melon and pushed up my throat, making it hard to breathe.

The bus was moving! It wasn't moving fast, but it was beginning to roll down the sloped road. I looked down at my feet, trying to understand what had happened. Somehow I must have kicked something important. I jammed my feet against the pedals, hoping that one of them would stop the bus. Two of the pedals were loose and the third was too tight to push. I kicked at them as the bus began to roll just a bit faster.

I looked out the front window. I was moments away from hitting the back of the bus parked in front of me. I held my breath and braced for the impact.

My bus knocked into the back of the second one. For a moment it felt like I had stopped. I was just about to breathe a sigh of relief when the bus in front of me began to roll and mine followed suit. The impact had knocked the brakes loose and now we were both moving. Everyone stopped banging on the outside of the bus and stepped back to scream.

"Stop this instant!" Squall squawked. "Stop this!"

He was welcome to yell until he was blue in the face, but I had no control over what was now transpiring. The bus in front of me rammed into the bus in front of it and it too began to move. All three vehicles were now beginning to pick up speed as we rolled down the slope of the road and straight toward the edge of Lake Mend.

I grabbed at the steering wheel and twisted violently to see if I could turn the bus away from what was happening, but the wheel was locked and the buses were really beginning to pick up speed. I started kicking and pounding at every knob and pedal on the bus, but nothing helped. I looked down the aisle and out the back door. I could see everyone back by the museum. All of them were running down the road, chasing after the buses. The students had wide open mouths and were waving their hands in the air. I couldn't see Kate, but I imagined that she was probably hiding somewhere, embarrassed to even know me. I tried to open the door so I could jump out, but at the speed we were rolling it wouldn't open. I could see out the front window and the first bus was about to reach the dock on the edge of the lake.

"I'm dead," I moaned needlessly.

I watched the first bus roll right over the dock and plummet ten feet down into Lake Mend. I would have been really interested in how cool it looked, but my mind was preoccupied with the fact that the same thing was about to happen to me and the bus I was on. Knowing there was no way I could stop what was happening, I got up and ran down the aisle to the rear of the bus.

I heard the bus in front of me crashing over the dock and into the water. I ducked down between the two backseats as I felt my bus rumbling over the dock. A frightening second later, the front of my bus dropped, and the vehicle plunged into the water nose first. I bounced between two of the stiff padded seats as I pushed my legs up against the side window.

Water quickly began to fill the front of the bus as the back end poked out of the water. There was junk in our trunk and that junk was me. I pushed open the large rear door and climbed out as the bus filled up and went under. The water around me sucked off my shoes and pushed me four feet to the right.

I treaded cold water as my teeth shivered and my body pulsated. I looked up and could see heads beginning to pop over the edge of the broken dock. There was Professor Squall and Mr. M. There was my class, and there was Kate. It wasn't hard to notice the fact that not a single one of them had a look of sympathy on their faces. Wyatt was holding in a laugh, but Kate looked too mortified to be caring at the moment.

I spit out a bunch of water and yelled up at her. "At least it was memorable!"

Kate didn't look very grateful.

CHAPTER 4

I Want to Tell You

NEVER HAD I BEEN SO INSULTED—well, maybe *never* was too strong a word. I guess I was just surprised that Professor Squall and Mr. M seemed almost disappointed that I wasn't injured. I kept trying to point out what a miracle it was that I was okay, and how we should all breathe a sigh of relief over me not getting too hurt. But not a single person seemed to go for it. After I was pulled out of the cold water of Lake Mend, Kate hugged me but then stepped away before I could drag her further into this.

I didn't have any life-threatening injuries, but I did have a few bruises on my right arm and a scratch where I had scraped my head against the back door while climbing out of the sinking bus. Unfortunately, not even the sight of blood made anyone sympathetic toward my cause.

After Professor Squall and Wyatt helped me get back up onto the damaged dock, I turned around and looked down at the water. I could barely see the three large yellow blobs beneath the lake's surface. Professor Squall squinted at the sunken buses and then turned to stare at me. His face was so red I was afraid he was going to just spontaneously combust and I'd be covered with bits of his bald head and white angry face.

"I—" I tried to say.

"You," Professor Squall squealed. "Those buses . . . that display . . . I'm . . ."

"Thankful I'm alive?" I asked.

Professor Squall put his head into his hands and moaned. He sounded like a sick whale. If Lake Mend actually had been home to any sea monsters or squids, they would have come jumping out of the water at the sound of his call.

Mr. M pushed through the crowd. He was waving his tiny hands in the air and screaming in frustration. He pointed at me.

"You!"

I was much more popular than I had thought.

"The display!" he continued. "You've destroyed priceless history! Wiggendale has been damaged."

"It was an accident," I argued.

A short woman put a blue fuzzy blanket over my shoulders.

I hadn't realized but I was shaking like a dryer filled with wet shoes. I could hear sirens and the sound of cars coming to a quick stop behind the crowd. Doors slammed, and four police officers worked their way through the group of students and rubberneckers to get to me. I recognized one of them.

"Beck," Sheriff Pax said with much too little surprise.

"Sheriff," I replied, wishing I were anywhere but here at the moment.

Sheriff Pax and I had a bit of history. Not too long ago I had accidentally taken the queen dragon out for a ride. I had flown over the mountains behind the manor, and Lizzy had spotted a small church with a tin roof. Dragons being how they are, with their love of all things shiny, Lizzy had descended on the church and torn part of the roof off. In doing so, the roof had mistakenly caught on fire and burned the church down, almost killing an old lady organist. There were no other witnesses, but Sheriff Pax had been pretty certain that I had something to do with it.

"Why am I not surprised this involves you?" Sheriff Pax asked.

"How do you know I'm involved? Maybe I'm just an innocent bystander," I said through shivering teeth.

Sheriff Pax rubbed his chin with his right hand and

adjusted his cap with his left. His gray eyes locked on my brown ones and wouldn't let go. Finally he blinked.

"You blinked," I said lamely. "I win?"

Sheriff Pax was actually a fairly nice guy. He was big and burly with a thin mustache and a thick hide. It looked like he was bald, but I wasn't certain, seeing as I had never seen him without his hat on. The uniform he wore was a brown button-up shirt with even browner pants and black shoes. He had a gun hooked to his belt and a nightstick on the other side.

The crowd of students around us was growing noisy, so Sheriff Pax ordered them to head back to the museum. I turned and started to walk with them, but the sheriff grabbed me by the wet collar and pulled me back.

"You're staying here," he said calmly. "There are a few things we need to discuss."

"But my class," I argued, pointing toward Kate and Wyatt and the rest of my classmates as they were walking back up the slight hill to Wiggendale. "I'm not supposed to be separated from my class."

"I think they know where you are," Sheriff Pax said.

"But if they do a head count they'll be one short," I said anxiously, not wanting to have to talk to the law. "And Professor Squall goes nuts whenever the count is short. He hates recounting because of the time it takes . . ."

"Beck," Sheriff Pax interrupted with authority, treating me as if I were a hysterical woman who had just seen a mouse and couldn't get my emotions under control. "Calm yourself."

My shoulders dropped, and I tried to catch my breath. A couple of other cops started toward us, but Sheriff Pax waved them away and then put his big arm around my shoulder.

"Let's take a walk, shall we? I want to talk to you about something."

I think he was trying to sound nice, but it actually sounded pretty sinister. Walks with grown-ups never end well. I was sort of worried that I might never come back from where we were heading.

"Come on," he insisted, not giving me a choice.

I started to walk with him. After ten steps he still hadn't said anything. Ten steps more and nothing. Apparently my demise was going to be silent. After twelve more steps I couldn't take it.

"I'm sure you have better things to do than stroll along with me," I reasoned. "I'm happy to just walk the rest of the way alone to wherever it is we're going."

Sheriff Pax sighed. We stopped walking, and he took his arm off my shoulder. He turned to look me directly in the eyes. The thin mustache above his lip twitched slightly. I was no stranger to the law. I had met a few police officers in my life. When I lived out west, there were a number of times when the things I had done caused the cops to take notice. Most of the police officers I had met were strict and overly disappointed in me being me. It always seemed like they were sad that a kid like me was freely walking around. Sheriff Pax was slightly different, however. And the people of Kingsplot liked him a lot. I had once heard Millie say that he was just the right mix of helping hand and iron fist.

"It was an accident," I said sincerely, breaking the silence that had been smothering the two of us like a thin plastic bag.

"Beck, your family—" Sheriff Pax stopped himself from saying more.

"I know, I know," I said dejectedly. "My family's got a few issues, but I didn't mean for those buses to do that. It seems like maybe the parking brakes on those things were faulty. Do you think I should sue?"

"Let's see," Sheriff Pax said lightly. "You break a museum display, cause a panic in a public place, commandeer a school bus and then drive it and two others over a dock and into a lake, and you're blaming the brakes and want to sue?"

"I'm pretty sure I have ADHD," I tried.

"That might very well be the case, but there are millions who do and have still never driven a bus off a dock."

"It was an accident," I tried again.

"Beck, this isn't the first trouble you've created."

He obviously wasn't about to let the past rest peacefully. Some people had the hardest time letting go of things.

"Really, I—" I tried to say.

Sheriff Pax held up one of his big hands to stop me. "Listen, Beck, I know you might not believe me, but I understand you better than you might think."

"Good," I said relieved. "Actually, maybe you could explain myself to me because I'm really confused."

Sheriff Pax almost smiled.

"What happened today was bad," the sheriff whistled, "really bad, but I feel like I should tell you something."

I gulped accordingly.

"When I was a kid," he continued, "I accidentally killed a turtle."

It was not what I expected him to say, but suddenly I was *way* more interested in the conversation we were having.

"Really, a turtle?" I asked.

"Actually, it was a tortoise."

"I don't know the difference," I admitted.

"My class took a field trip to the Kingsplot Zoo," the sheriff went on. "There used to be an extremely old tortoise that walked around the zoo. Kids could touch it or get their picture taken by it."

"That sounds amazing," I said, trying to sound excited.

Sheriff Pax rubbed his forehead. "That's not the point," he continued. "I'd always been curious about whether a tortoise really could get stuck on its back. So while the tortoise was walking by our class, I reached down and grabbed the right side of its shell. I then pulled it up and flipped it onto its back."

"And?" I prodded.

"Well, I flipped it so hard that it rolled all the way over and then kept rolling down the hill on the edge of the path. It tumbled and crashed into a stone wall that surrounded the ostrich pen."

"Wow," I whispered. "Then what?"

"Well, there were no more 'then whats' for that turtle," Sheriff Pax said.

"It was dead?" I chattered.

Sheriff Pax nodded. "The zoo had a funeral four days later. All the businesses of Kingsplot shut down for the day, and I was banished from going near another living animal for five years."

"Wow," I said softly, a new appreciation for Sheriff Pax growing in my soul. "That's worse than ruining a few buses."

"Nice try," Sheriff Pax said. "That turtle was beloved, but it was on its last leg. I shouldn't have done that, but what you did was far worse. You could have hurt or killed a number of people. You could have killed yourself. What if someone had been in front of the buses or on the dock?"

"I prefer to point out the fact that nobody was," I pointed out.

"Beck, there will be repercussions," Sheriff Pax said sternly. "We will need to take you to the police station for a little bit."

"But you understand, right?" I argued. "I mean, you knocked off a tortoise, and I only ruined a field trip to the museum."

"It's not that easy."

"Can't we just have a funeral for the buses?" I said frantically. "I promise I'll cry in public so everyone can see how bad I feel. I'll even write one of those sad poems that people write to convey how sorry they are. 'Today we all make quite a fuss, because we lost our dear old bus.' See?"

"I need you to come with me to the police station," the sheriff said calmly.

"But you're just like me, remember?" I pleaded.

"Beck, I didn't tell you that story to give you an out," Sheriff Pax said compassionately. "I told you that story so that as you experience what is about to happen you might realize that it won't be comfortable for either of us."

"But . . ."

Sheriff Pax pointed down with his right hand and whirled his finger, signaling for me to turn around.

I turned around, questioning what was happening as it was

happening. "Why do you need me to turn around?" I was suddenly scared that he might kick me in the butt and send me back over the edge of the lake and into the water.

"Hands behind your back," the sheriff said.

I put my hands behind my back and felt something cold slip up against my wrists, and then I heard the handcuffs click closed.

"You have the right to remain silent—" Sheriff Pax told me my rights and then turned me around and marched me back toward his car.

I couldn't believe what was happening to me. Sure, a lot of odd things had occurred since I had moved to Kingsplot. I had raised dragons, discovered my father, and destroyed a few things along the way, but this was the first time I had been arrested.

We reached the cop car, and a short woman cop with really awful teeth opened the rear door so that Sheriff Pax could push me into the backseat. My arms burned as I sat back against my shackled hands. Sheriff Pax closed the door and then climbed into the driver's seat. He looked back at me through a wire divider that separated the backseat from the front. His big eyes were cold and almost as metallic as the ball bearings I had *accidentally* set loose.

"I—" I tried to explain.

"Save it," Sheriff Pax stopped me. He then swiveled his head, turned on the car, and drove away.

Two things bothered me. One, I was being arrested for something that had been a complete accident. And two, Sheriff Pax didn't even have the courtesy to turn on his siren and make the ride back to the police station a little more exciting.

We drove past the museum and I could see all of my fellow students standing around the front of it, most likely waiting for new buses to come and take them away. I could see Kate standing by Wyatt. She looked up as we drove by. Since my hands were bound behind me, I waved with my head. Kate shook hers in reply. Professor Squall was frantically trying to keep everyone in order. I hoped he had a really hard go at it. After all, this field trip was his idea. If this was what I got for finishing my work on time, I decided that I'm going to start turning things in late.

Some great reward.

The year 1751 in Scotland was a time of great importance to the Pillage family. Happiness and success were clearly on the horizon. Sorrow seemed the worry of others, and others

The beginning of section one of The Grim Knot

CHAPTER 5

Every Little Thing

KINGSPLOT'S POLICE STATION WAS located in one of the old structures near the center of town. It was an interesting square building with a ring of ornate stone molding that ran around the top of its third story. The windows were tall and skinny, and there was a massive granite eave that jutted out over the front door. On top of the eave were two naked stone angels with wings and sashes. Beneath the angels were the words *order* and *peace*.

Sheriff Pax walked me through the front doors and over to a row of short desks near a painting of a flock of birds. The birds looked as if they were trying to fly out of the frame they were trapped in.

I sat down on the edge of a gray plastic chair and hung my head to give the appearance of humility. Sheriff Pax asked me a few questions and filled out a couple of forms. He then took off my handcuffs and allowed me to call home. I picked up the phone on his desk and dialed the manor. Millie answered.

"Millie, it's me," I said.

There was a short pause. Sheriff Pax looked away and pretended to be busy with something else.

"Millie, I . . ."

"I've heard," she spoke, without letting me finish.

"Heard what?" I asked.

"Every little thing," she scolded. "Beck, there's too much Pillage coursing through your blood."

"Exactly," I agreed. "I blame my ancestors also. Could you send Thomas to get me?"

"Thomas isn't here," Millie reported.

"Wane?" I asked. "Could you send Wane to bail me out?"

"She's unavailable," Millie informed me.

"Scott?"

"He's gone."

"You?"

"I never learned how to drive," Millie reminded me. "There are stations in life, Beck. I know my place is in the kitchen. I leave the driving to others."

"Right," I said, bothered. "What about my dad?"

"What about him?" she asked. "He's still in the hospital; you know that."

The hospital that Millie was talking about wasn't a regular hospital. Many months ago my father had been moved to the "special" hospital where he was working on being able to think properly again. I knew it was the nut house, but everyone just called it the hospital as if he were there to be treated for a broken leg or a bad case of the flu.

"Well," I said, extremely bothered now. "Someone needs to come bail me out. I can't spend the night here."

"There are worse things than jail," Millie informed me. "Besides, the Kingsplot facilities are some of the finest in the world."

Really irritated now, and getting a little worried, I was still sidetracked enough by her response to ask, "How do you know?"

"Beck, we'll send for you as soon as possible."

"Can't you ..."

"Do you realize what you did?"

"Yes," I sighed. "I was there."

"Then you should know that there are consequences and details we need to work out before we can get you back."

"It wasn't my fault," I said, wondering why nobody in the

world understood that. I looked at Sheriff Pax as he continued to act as if he weren't listening.

"People have accidents. Sheriff Pax killed a turtle," I argued irrationally.

"I remember," Millie said, suddenly sounding very sad. "That was a dark time for Kingsplot. But Sheriff Pax's history is not yours. Who knows how many fish you killed with those buses?"

"Fish?" I shouted.

"Lake Mend is a beautiful lake, and now it's littered with those machines you destroyed. Machines your family will have to pay for."

Millie made it sound as though I had intentionally slaughtered a few giant robots and tossed them into the lake to poop oil all over the fish.

"It was an accident," I repeated, sounding like a guilty parrot.

"Beck, Thomas is quite disappointed," Millie said softly. "Quite disappointed. And poor Scott, well, he had to sit down when he heard the news."

This call was going far worse than I had anticipated. I knew I would be in trouble, and I figured there would be a bit of swearing and perhaps punishment that involved pulling weeds around the property or having to write a letter of apology to the museum. What I hadn't expected was the guilt being administered in such heavy doses.

"Wane cried," Millie added. "And your father—"

Millie let her words drift off into an uncomfortable silence.

"Did you tell him?" I finally asked.

"Thomas had to," Millie informed me. "He's responsible for you. Those buses will take a considerable sum of money to replace."

"I'm sorry," I said as sincerely and honestly as I possibly could. "Really, Millie, I'm sorry."

I could hear Millie sigh deeply. She groaned just a little and then spoke. "The Pillage name is something to honor, not destroy."

I wanted to point out that every Pillage before me had spent far more time destroying than honoring our family name, but I let it go.

"Will you come get me?" I asked in complete earnestness.

"In time," Millie answered. "In time."

I cupped my hand over the phone and turned as far away from Sheriff Pax as I could. In a whisper I said, "You don't understand, Millie. Tell my dad that mushrooms were trying to get me." I had not told Millie about how much plants hated me, but I wanted out badly enough that I thought I would let her in on my problem.

"What?" Millie asked, as if I had suddenly started speaking another language.

"Mushrooms," I whispered. "Plants have been attacking me."

"Beck, this is nonsense," Millie insisted.

"My dad will understand," I pleaded. "Will you send someone to get me?"

"In time," Millie said again.

There was a soft click as she hung up the phone. I sat there listening to the silent receiver. I felt so different from the kid that had wandered into Kingsplot all that time ago. I was taller, stronger, and my brown hair was finally long enough to look properly shaggy. My ears didn't stick out as much and my brown eyes looked darker. Of course, no amount of hair or height could change the fact that I was still a walking mess. I wanted to be like other kids my age. I wanted to stress out about normal teenage things like acne and being accepted. I thought about how comforting it would be to simply worry about who liked who or how grown-ups were messing up the world that would someday be ours. Instead, my life was filled with dragons and destruction, and I was constantly turning things like field trips into long, painful, drawn-out life lessons.

I hung up the phone and looked at Sheriff Pax.

"Millie said you need to just let me go," I tried.

"Really?" Sheriff Pax said, not buying it for a second.

"Yeah, so I'll just see myself out."

I tried to stand up, but the way the sheriff was staring at me frightened my legs, and they refused to move.

"Maybe I'll just stay awhile," I gave up.

"That sounds like a better idea," Sheriff Pax said almost kindly.

A couple of other cops came in and reported on a few things. They also told Sheriff Pax how it would be next to impossible to get those buses out of the lake. All three of them then looked at me and shook their heads.

Sheriff Pax instructed a skinny officer to take me away. I was placed in a small iron jail cell in the basement of the police department. There were three other jail cells, but they were all empty. The skinny officer handed me some clothes and instructed me to change into them. I took the clothes, but I had no intention of ever wearing them.

"We haven't locked anyone up in months," the skinny cop told me as I stepped into the cell.

"I feel really special," I replied.

I think my words caused him to slam my cell door much harder than was necessary.

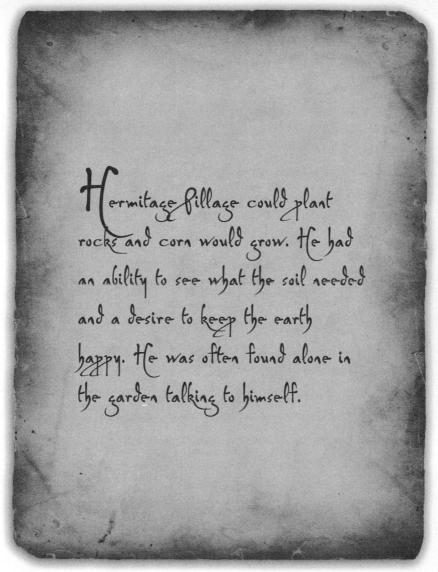

Hermitage Pillage could plant rocks and corn would grow. He had an ability to see what the soil needed and a desire to keep the earth happy. He was often found alone in the garden talking to himself.

The beginning of section two of The Grim Knot

CHAPTER 6

A Really Hard Day's Night

SURPRISINGLY, THE CELL I WAS in was clean and didn't look like any jail cell I had ever seen on TV before. There was a nice twin bed with two big fluffy pillows and a toilet in the corner behind a privacy wall. Near the front of the cell was a white sink and faucet. There was also a small end table that was bolted to the ground. Above the table was a light switch that turned on a round fluorescent ceiling light above the bed. When I squinted and pretended the bars were just long shadows the place almost looked cozy. It didn't feel as confining as my own room at the manor because I could see out into the other empty cells and down the hallway to the office door. There was also a tiny high window that let a little bit of daylight in.

At first I thought that having to stay the night wouldn't be so bad—it's not like I was new to being held captive—I had been locked up in my room in the manor a number of times. But after a few hours, I was so bored I wanted out. At least when I was locked up in the manor, I had *The Grim Knot* to study and try to figure out. Here I had nothing but a pile of clothes I refused to change into. I thought about confessing to things I had never done just to get the chance to talk to someone besides myself.

Around five Sheriff Pax came and took me to a small room with a table and two chairs in it. I sat in one of the chairs while he questioned me. He asked about the museum display I had ruined and about the bus. He wanted to know if I had planned to do what I had done or if it had all been spontaneous. When I told him it was very much a spontaneous act, he began to question me about the mushrooms. His new line of questioning caught me off guard. I hadn't figured out yet just what I was going to say about the crazy fungi that had popped up in Wiggendale Museum. Professor Squall had scared them off, and now I was left wondering what they had been trying to tell me. Sheriff Pax asked me about them again. I decided to just be honest.

"What mushrooms?" I asked.

"Come on, Beck," Sheriff Pax said, suspiciously. "The main museum room was littered with huge mushrooms. Those didn't look spontaneous. Are you saying you didn't plan that out and bring them in?"

"You think I planned some sort of mushroom hoax? I laughed. "I don't even like mushrooms; ask Millie or Thomas."

"Beck, this is no joke," Sheriff Pax said. "Are you saying you didn't bring them in?"

"I guess that's what I'm saying," I answered.

Sheriff Pax smiled and then stared at me. He was obviously playing the role of both good cop and bad cop at the same time. "So you have nothing to say about the mushrooms?"

"They're disgusting?" I tried.

He asked me a few more questions, told me I needed to change into the clothes they had given me, and then led me back to my cell.

"Is Thomas coming?" I asked with concern.

"Not tonight," Sheriff Pax replied. "Now change into the clothes we gave you. You still smell like Lake Mend. You might as well make yourself comfortable; you could be here a couple of days."

"But I—" I had nothing to say. I wanted to whine and argue, but there were no words I could have thrown out that felt strong enough to break me out of this mess.

Sheriff Pax escorted me to my cell and turned the key.

"We'll turn the lights out in an hour," he informed me. "You have one in your cell if you need it."

"Can't I just go home and think about what I've done?" I begged. "I promise I'll think really hard."

"See you in the morning, Beck," Sheriff Pax replied. "There are two officers up front who will check on you through the night."

Sheriff Pax walked down the hall and out the door. He shut the door behind him, and I could hear it too being locked.

"Perfect," I grumbled, while sitting down on the bed. "Some field trip. Education's the worst."

I looked up at the tiny barred window and could see the light of day turning gray. I had nothing to do. There wasn't a single thing to read or study. There was no TV or smart phone or radio or even graffiti to look at. I lay back on the bed and closed my eyes. I knew my dad would never let this slide. He was sick, but he wasn't so sick that he couldn't think up a punishment that would mess up my life for a while. It was always a little disconcerting to be punished by someone who lacked discipline in their own life. My adopted mother used to always tell me to be honest and work hard, when she had a hard time telling the truth and had spent her days sleeping.

I ran my hands through my hair and shook my head like a dog wanting to shake off water. I was so frustrated by what I had done. Lately I had been getting more and more bothered by myself and some of the things I accidentally did. Now here

I was locked up with nobody but myself. I was in the mood for better company.

"Great," I mumbled.

I stood up and walked to the cell door. I grabbed two of the bars and pulled. It was locked tight. I yelled down the hall hoping they would hear me out in the front office.

"Hey!" I hollered. "Hey, police people!"

There was no sound or indication that I had been heard. I decided to yell louder.

"Police guys! Can I get a magazine, or a book, or a TV, or someone sane enough to let me go home?"

Nothing.

I sat back down on my bed and took off my shoes. I pulled off my socks. My feet were still wrinkled from the surprise swim I had taken earlier. I suddenly wished I could take a shower. I thought about yelling some more and demanding that they let me shower, but I wasn't that sure about whether or not I wanted to take a shower at a police station.

I picked up the pile of clothes I had been given and unfolded them. There was a long, one-piece jumpsuit that had black and white stripes running horizontally. It looked just like the prison suits you saw prisoners in old photos wearing. There was no way I was ever going to put it on. I could see it now; someone would get a picture of me wearing it, and then years from now, when I wanted to run for president of the world, that picture would show up and ruin my sterling reputation. There was also a black-and-white striped nightcap. I actually laughed out loud when I realized what it was. It looked exactly like the kind of thing a criminal elf would wear. A pair of big, stark-white socks and some tighty-whiteys completed the ensemble. There was no way I was going to put on underwear that belonged to the cops. I set the bundle of clothes on the floor and lay down on the bed.

I stared at the washed-out concrete ceiling and thought of all the people who would someday feel bad about me being locked up. There was a knock at the far door down the hallway, but when I yelled for whoever it was to come in, nobody did.

I didn't think I was tired, but the excitement of the day and the accident that had dragged me into the lake must have taken it out of me. My eyelids struggled to keep open. After a couple of attempts at keeping them up, I let them snap shut, and sleep smothered me like a heavy beanbag.

I'm not sure how long I slept, but when I woke up it was pitch-black. It took me a few moments to figure out where I was. When I realized that I was in jail and that the field trip had not just been a nightmare, I sat up and moaned.

I slid off of my bed and felt my way over to the wall, where I flipped the switch and turned on the small, round fluorescent light on the ceiling. A weak blue light hummed like a fat pasty face staring down at me. The light barely lit up my small cell.

I was supposed to be old and brave, but at the moment I felt young for my age and slightly bothered by how little I could see. The air was still, and I could smell something that reminded me of stale food. I looked around and realized that there was a tray of food on the edge of the sink. Apparently someone had come in and dropped it off while I was sleeping. I picked up the tray and carried it over to my bed. I set it down on the end and then sat cross-legged in front of it. The light wasn't strong enough for me to be able to tell just what kind of meat was on the sandwich, so the first bite was a gamble. I chewed, determined it was ham, and then finished the whole thing in four more bites. I downed the small bowl of fruit and the brownie that tasted like it had peanut butter in it. The food wasn't quite as good as Millie's, but it wasn't bad. I set my tray back on the sink and belched in a way that only someone who was alone in a prison cell would dare.

"Excuse me," I said to myself.

The buzzing blue light above me flickered spastically. I looked up at the small window, wishing that Kate would break through and bust me out.

Vwisst!

I swatted at my left ear as a small bug flew past. I looked

around in the dark, wondering where the pest had gone and
what kind of bug it was.

Vwisst!

It buzzed near my right ear, and I ducked quickly to the left.
It was one thing to have it be so dark, but it was another thing
altogether to be sharing the dark with some unknown insect.
Bad memories of the time I had spent stuck in a furnace vent
with a bag full of bees washed over me.

Vwisst! Wiffft!

I spun around like an awkward ballerina, trying to catch a
glimpse of what was flying around. I stepped over to the tray
with my dirty dishes and pushed off the dishes. I picked up the
empty tray.

Vwisst! Wiffft! Wiffft!

I swung the tray around like a giant flyswatter, batting
at whatever was after me. I could hear something small click
up against the swinging tray. I crouched down in the corner
and stared at the front of the cell. Whatever was pestering me
seemed to be coming from the direction of the door, and the
tiny bit of light in my cell barely reached out past the bars.

Vwisst! Wiffft! Piffff!

"Ouch!"

Something stung me on the right elbow. I slapped at my

arm, and whatever had bit me jammed into my hand, stinging it as well.

I looked at my hand. I could see a long, thin stinger sticking out of my index finger.

"What the . . . ?"

I didn't have time to question what I had found because the sudden sound of something expanding filled the air. That sound was followed by an assault of whizzing projectiles flying through the air. I could feel hundreds of needles stinging my legs and arms. The tray had protected my face and chest, but my gut now looked like the back end of a porcupine. I yelled as loud as I could, hoping that one of the policemen would hurry up and come to my rescue.

I could hear something expanding again. I turned to the side as hundreds of needles flew through the air and poked through my clothes and into the back of my head. None of them went deep enough to do any real harm, but they stung. I looked like an acupuncture test dummy.

I swatted and pulled at the needles while grabbing the mattress off my bed and scurrying behind it. Just as I made it behind the mattress, the sound of something expanding again filled the air. One moment later I heard the sound of thousands of needles hitting the other side of the mattress. I screamed and screamed until I realized I was embarrassing myself. I rubbed all the needles off my arms and from the back of my head and then stayed huddled behind the mattress listening to myself breathe.

The air was completely still.

After a few minutes of silence I tried yelling for help once more—once more, nobody came to my aid. After a few minutes more I pushed the mattress up and moved to peer carefully out of the side.

I couldn't see anything outside the bubble of weak light.

Scattered all over the ground were thousands of thin needles. They were also poking out of the mattress and sticking to the walls. I pulled some out of my shirt and looked at them closely. They were all about an inch and a half long with a sharp clear end.

I looked out toward the cell door, listening anxiously for the sound of anything expanding and holding the tray over my head. I couldn't see anything but black. I tried to calm my breathing and get my wits about me.

Srrrrwwwit.

Something huge shuffled closer and stood directly in front of the cell door. I screamed in a manner not very becoming of a boy my age.

Standing directly in front of the door was a seven-foot-tall cactus. It had two arms sticking out from its right side and one from its left. The bottom was chewed up and worn down as if it had dragged itself a great distance to get where it now was. There were only a few needles still on it.

The cactus pushed closer to the bars and the sound of it expanding once more filled the air. I ducked back behind the mattress as the cactus shot out its last remaining quills. It then began banging up against the outside of the cell as if trying to get in.

"Help!" I yelled as loud as I could. "Somebody!"

I looked out from behind the mattress and could see the huge thick cactus heaving itself up against the bars, trying to get into my space. Luckily, it was too big to fit through. It also looked to now be completely needle free. It had shot out all of its weapons and now wanted in to finish me off.

"Get away!" I hollered, as if it were possible to reason with a cactus. "Guards!"

Still nobody came, and the large cactus appeared to be getting angrier as it violently thrust its entire body against the bars. I looked up at the tiny light, wishing it would try harder to be bright. It was still too dark to really feel any sort of hope or fully make out what was happening.

One of the cactus's right arms pushed through the bars, reaching directly toward me. I was too far away for it to actually touch me, but it didn't make me happy in the least. I stood up and began hitting it as hard as I could with the food tray. The tray chipped away at the thick, spongy cactus, sending chunks of it all over. I turned the tray and began to chop at the arm like it was a log.

The torso of the cactus was pushing up against the bars so hard that parts of it were beginning to squish through. I took one more whack at the arm and it sliced off and fell to the ground.

"Help!" I continued to scream.

I flipped the tray around and began to jab at the body of the cactus with one of the corners. The tray created gashes and caused the plant to pull back just a bit. I took that as a positive sign to continue. I went wild with the jabbing, and the cactus pulled back even farther. I thought for a brief second that I was winning, but it just shivered and began to hurl itself at the bars with such force that it was beginning to break apart. Chunks, wads, and fistfuls were tearing off and falling to the floor as it continued its rant of self-destruction. Its left arm worked through the bars, and I sliced it off with two blows. It was so torn and beat up that the entire plant was beginning to just crumble and fall to the ground. I continued to hack at it through the bars, still screaming for help and wondering what I had done in some previous lifetime to cause this—what horrible heinous crime against plants had I been a part of to bring this on?

The very top of the cactus broke off, followed by the last remaining arm. I shoved the tray through the bars and split the center of the cactus. It busted open like a vegetarian piñata—bits of sticky cactus falling to the ground and settling on the floor.

I dropped the tray and fell to my knees. My body was exhausted. I had red prickly marks all over my arms from where I had been repeatedly pricked. I also still had needles in my hair and clothes, making it painful and awkward to move or sit down.

"Thanks for the help!" I yelled.

I gazed at the chewed-up pile of cactus and wondered where it had come from. It looked a lot like the one I had seen at Wiggendale. And since there weren't many cacti in Kingsplot, I had to believe that's where this one had come from.

My heart was racing so fast I was afraid it was going to slip up out of my mouth and fall to the floor in the cactus heap. I was just about to stand up when one of the chunks of cactus twitched.

I did a double take and noticed that the first arm I had severed was rising up from the pile of its slaughtered body.

"No!" I yelled. "Guards!"

I picked up the tray as more and more of the small pieces began to shiver and shake toward me, working their way through the bars and gaining momentum. My body ached, and my mind felt like a punching bag that a twitchy boxer was repeatedly punching.

I couldn't imagine how things could be worse.

Apparently I need to work on my imagination. As I was hyperventilating and watching my life flash before my eyes, the overhead light buzzed twice and then flickered off, leaving me completely in the dark.

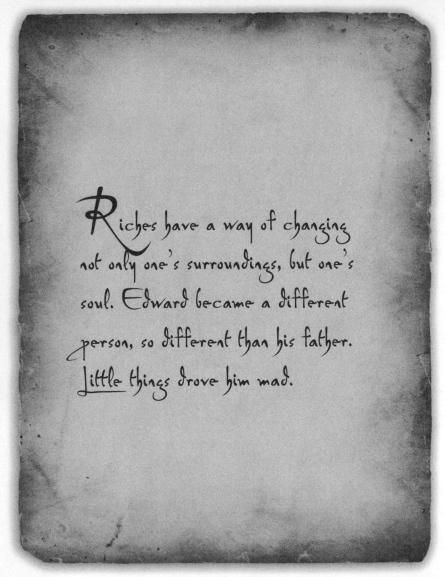

Riches have a way of changing not only one's surroundings, but one's soul. Edward became a different person, so different than his father. Little things drove him mad.

The beginning of section three of The Grim Knot

CHAPTER 7

Please, Mister Policeman

FEAR PUMPED THROUGH MY BLOOD—my cell was completely dark. I couldn't see my hand in front of my face, and all I could hear was the sound of my heart dry heaving and big, sticky chunks of rabid cactus sliding toward me.

"Guards!"

Nobody was coming to my rescue. I felt something brush up against my right leg, and I completely lost it. I began twirling and screaming and batting that tray up against everything and anything that dared get in front of me.

Not being able to see my feet, I slipped, causing my body to slam into the sink and bounce against the bars. I ignored the pain and continued to fight valiantly against the oncoming cactus carcass. Chunks were swirling and moving around my legs. I tripped over the mattress and fell onto my stomach. I was instantly bombarded with cactus wreckage. I could feel bits of it covering most of my body.

I tried to shift and beat pieces off me with the tray, but there were just too many. Some chunks were now trying to shove themselves into my mouth and eyes. I was in the mood to scream a little more, but I was afraid to open my lips for fear of cactus getting in.

I kicked and flailed, but it was no use, I was being beat down. Everything was sticky and painful. A large piece pushed into my right eye, and the sting was so sharp I couldn't stop myself from shrieking.

The second my mouth opened, cactus flowed in. My throat burned, and I began to heave and cough, spewing pieces of the plant all over. I was seconds from consigning myself to death when lights flashed on and I could hear the hallway door opening up. Like the mushrooms I had tangled with earlier, every last bit of cactus froze and dropped to the ground.

"Sweet Jane!" the skinny cop said, running up to my cell. His eyes were as wide as saucers, and he had his hand on his nightstick as if it might be needed. He looked into my cell and stared at me as I lay there covered in needles and cactus remains.

I was so happy he had interrupted my death that I smiled.

Unfortunately, he didn't smile back. I was glad to be alive, but I knew beyond any doubt that somehow this cop was going to think this was my fault. The officer began to swear like it was part of the cop oath to do so. He opened up the cell door and yanked me up. He had more questions than I had answers.

"What the . . . ? How is it possible . . . ? Why would you . . . ? Do you think this is acceptable?"

"No," was all I could say.

The officer informed me that it was after one in the morning and that I was now in more trouble than I had ever been. He took me from my cell back to the front office of the police station. There was only one other officer in the building with us at the time. I got cleaned up, and I happily put on a needle-free, black-and-white striped jumpsuit. It's funny how people's taste in fashion changes with time and circumstances. They put me in one of the other cells, and the skinny officer put a chair right outside my door and took a seat.

"I'm going to sit here until the sun rises," he said angrily. "I'll have my eyes on you, so no more funny business."

There was no way I wanted to be left alone, so I used a little strategy I had learned in dealing with the folks at the manor.

"You don't have to stay," I said. "Go on."

I knew that adults sometimes needed to be prodded into sticking to their decisions. Going against a kid's wishes was often the final encouragement they needed. The last thing I wanted was to be by myself again. I didn't feel like I would ever be safe until every last plant was locked up.

"Seriously," I added. "I'll be fine by myself."

"Nice try, kid," the officer said. "I'm not letting you out of my sight. Understand?"

"Yes," I said, sounding sad but feeling thankful.

"When Sheriff Pax gets here and sees the mess you made, you'll have some real explaining to do."

I didn't reply. Instead I lay down and partook of some real sleeping.

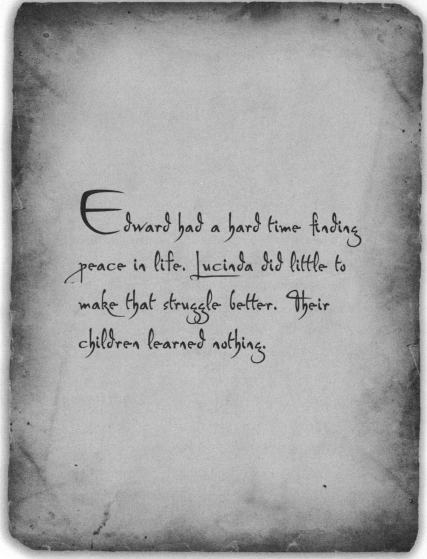

Edward had a hard time finding peace in life. Lucinda did little to make that struggle better. Their children learned nothing.

The beginning of section four of The Grim Knot

CHAPTER 8

Ask Me Why

O NLY I COULD GET ATTACKED BY a cactus and then get in trouble for it. The entire police station was mad at me for making such a mess.

I was checked over by doctors, grilled by officers, and ignored by my family. I thought for sure that Thomas would come immediately after Sheriff Pax told him about the cactus attack, but no.

Sheriff Pax and his officers were pretty baffled by what had happened. The afternoon after it took place, Sheriff Pax pulled me into his office, locked the door behind us, closed his blinds, and put his phone in his drawer so that it wouldn't bother us.

I didn't think that preparation bode well for me.

Sheriff Pax took a seat on the edge of his desk while I sat in a red leather chair directly in front of it. He sighed, rubbed his eyes, and then sighed again. If he was hoping to break me down with that, he was way off. I had had very few conversations with adults in my life that didn't begin with them sighing and rubbing their furrowed brows.

"Can we talk honestly, Beck?" he asked.

"I'm a big fan of honesty," I said, sitting up straight in my black-and-white striped jumpsuit. My arms and parts of my head were speckled with tiny red marks that the cactus quills had inflicted.

"I'm baffled," Sheriff Pax said.

"I think it's admirable that you would admit that."

Sheriff Pax shook his head. "Is everything a joke to you, Beck?"

"Not everything," I said nicely. "I don't think Professor Squall's funny."

"My point exactly," Sheriff Pax grumbled. "I want to help you, Beck. I even think you know that, but some things about you are very difficult to explain."

"I'm not really that complicated," I pointed out.

"Really?" he questioned. "Do you know how many mushrooms they cleaned up over at the museum?"

"Ten?"

"Thousands," he corrected. "They were all over the place

and in all sizes. Some were growing out of the walls and some from the small traces of mold along the baseboards."

"They really should keep that place cleaner," I commented. "Besides, I already told you that I didn't bring in those mushrooms."

"Right," the sheriff conceded. "Do you want to hear something else strange?"

"Not if it's about you personally," I said.

Sheriff Pax grumbled softly.

"Sorry," I apologized.

"Listen, Beck," he pushed on. "I'm not quite sure what happened here last night. I don't think I've ever seen a more gruesome scene."

"The death of a cactus is never an easy thing."

He ignored my remark and asked, "So you still have no idea what happened?"

"I told you. I was sleeping, and when I woke up there were needles and pieces of cactus everywhere," I lied. "I thought you and your men were just playing a joke on me. You know, like an initiation, or police brutality."

"Really?" the sheriff asked suspiciously. "So you're sticking to your story?"

I nodded.

"You know, I've been doing some checking," Sheriff Pax

said, standing up. "When you first arrived here there were some reports from your school of oddities."

"That's just Clark," I said, waving. "His eyes are too big for his head and they kind of bulge out a bit."

"Beck," Sheriff Pax said firmly.

"Sorry."

"The oddities I'm speaking of have to do with plants," he continued. "There was mention of plants coming in through the school windows and picking kids up."

"That is odd," I replied.

Sheriff Pax took out a small notebook and flipped it open. "There was some sort of dustup in the school cafeteria," he read. "Salads were flying around."

"That was the heat ducts," I explained, using the same lame excuse the teachers had used when it happened.

"Stranger still is that over a year ago dragons attacked this town and people barely remember it."

"I haven't forgotten," I said, equally baffled by the short memories of those in Kingsplot.

"Yes," Sheriff Pax said slowly. "Here's the thing, I have lived in Kingsplot my whole life. I didn't even know there was anything out there beyond our valley until I was in high school."

"That might be the fault of your geography teacher. Was it old Professor Welsh?"

The sheriff ignored my remarks yet again. "I have never traveled beyond the Hagen Valley and I have no desire to," he continued. "Do you think that's weird?"

"Home is where the heart is," I said remembering the saying from an embroidered pillow I once saw.

"Beck, I think there's something wrong with our town," the sheriff confessed.

The mood in the room suddenly grew heavy. I could feel the air thin out, and a thick oppressive anxiety weighed down on both of us. It was as if, for the first time in his life, Sheriff Pax knew something was different with his town, and he had the presence of mind to recognize it.

"What are you talking about?" I asked with a nervous laugh, hoping to lighten things up.

"I think there might be something askew here, and I feel as if the only person who might truly understand what I'm talking about is you. I went back to the museum today because someone stole one of their cactuses—the biggest one—a saguaro that was shipped in from out West years ago. It had cost thousands of dollars, and it was the centerpiece of their cactus garden. You know the weird thing about that missing cactus?"

I shook my head, feeling as if he were trying to trick me into admitting something I didn't want to admit.

"I'll tell you the weird thing," he continued. "It doesn't look like anyone broke in and took that cactus. It looks like it just jumped out of the display where it was planted, dragged itself across the floor, and squeezed out through a small, high museum window."

"How can you tell that?" I asked nervously, while looking around for any other cactuses that might be thinking of bursting into the station and finishing me off.

"I can tell because there's a clear trail of dirt and needles and no sign of someone else," he answered. "Then, outside of the museum, there's a faint trail of needles and dirt leading across town and up to this station. I'm not the brightest bulb in the world, but I'm thinking that's the same cactus you tore up in your cell."

"I told you I didn't bring it in," I argued.

"Listen, Beck," Sheriff Pax insisted. "I feel like for the first time I'm waking up, and I can see that something isn't right here. Dragons aren't real; cacti don't walk across town. I'm an officer of the law, and those things don't make sense."

"I agree with you totally," I said supportively.

"Beck," Sheriff Pax snapped. "This is me being as honest with you as I can. What happened last night in your cell?"

I looked at Sheriff Pax carefully. He was staring at me so intently that I started talking and couldn't get my mouth to stop.

I told him about the mushrooms and the cactus and how I was scared of every living thing at the moment.

"So you can make things grow?" he asked incredulously.

"Sort of," I answered. "It's something in the Pillage blood. I think that's part of the reason my dad's so sick. Sometimes plants just seem to have minds of their own and a desire to pick on me."

Sheriff Pax was silent for a moment. He walked around his desk, peeked out the blinds on his window, and sat down in his desk chair. He sighed in a way that must have released every bit of air his body contained, and then shut his eyes. When he finally opened them back up, he seemed relieved to see me.

"There has to be some way for us to figure all of this out," the sheriff said. "If I forget or my mind grows foggy like all the others here, you have to remind me."

"I'll try," I said honestly, liking the idea of having a confidant who was also the law.

Sheriff Pax took me back to my cell without saying one more word to me.

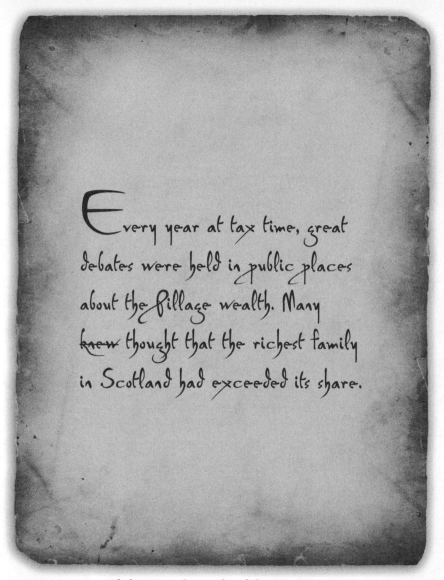

Every year at tax time, great debates were held in public places about the ~~fillage~~ village wealth. Many ~~knew~~ thought that the richest family in Scotland had exceeded its share.

The beginning of section five of The Grim Knot

CHAPTER 9

Chains

REALLY EARLY THE NEXT DAY, Thomas finally came to the station and picked me up. I was pretty happy to see him. Thomas was a tall man with thin shoulders and crooked legs. He had intensely dark eyes and a bulbous nose that looked as if it would work better on a Muppet.

Thomas paid my small bail and then led me to the car without saying a word. Because my clothes had been torn up and ruined by the rogue cactus, I had to leave the police station wearing my black-and-white striped jumpsuit.

The ride back to the manor was completely silent except for the occasional sound of Thomas clearing his throat and running his hands around the steering wheel with what I felt was an excessive amount of force.

The old blue Mercedes climbed up the steep roads through

the stone tunnels and into the high mountains. The air was wet, but strong beams of light broke through the clouds and put on a laser show as we ascended. At one point I reached to turn on the radio, but my actions were halted by a grunt from Thomas.

When we reached the gate to the manor, Thomas said, "Home, sweet home," as if he had read somewhere that saying that to a delinquent would help him out. The three gargoyles on top of the gatehouse stared down at us as we drove through.

As we passed the statues and the tall trees lining the drive, it felt good to be home.

We reached the stone fountain and courtyard. Thomas pulled the car up to the back door and shut off the engine. He turned to look at me, opened his mouth as if to speak, thought better of it, and then just shook his head.

"Did you have something to say?" I asked.

"Come," Thomas replied sadly.

I climbed out of the car and walked up to the large service door near the main kitchen. Thomas pushed the door open. Millie was in the kitchen beating the spunk out of a large wad of dough. She stopped harassing the dough the moment we walked in. She looked at me in my prison garb, and I could almost hear her heart break.

"Why do you have red marks all over?" she asked. "Does the jail have bedbugs?"

"They're from a cactus," I informed her.

"Oh, right," Millie said slowly. "Sheriff Pax told us about the incident."

"It was more than an incident," I insisted.

Millie sighed.

Maybe it was just me, but she seemed to have aged since I had come to the Pillage manor—of course, that aging was most likely because of me. On a normal day she was one of the nicest people I knew. She cared for me like a mother and grandmother combined. She was short and plump and by far the best cook I had ever met. Her meals were the sort of creations Zeus probably ate when he was really celebrating.

Millie had never told me her age, but if I had to guess, I'd say she was somewhere over fifty-five and below eighty. She walked with a slight limp and tilted just a tiny bit to the right nowadays. She also had a lazy right eye and was carrying around twenty pounds over the doctor-recommended weight for a person her height. I loved Millie. Usually I could talk her into anything by simply smiling correctly, but I could see that even my best smile wasn't going to save me today. I tried anyway. Millie scowled in return.

"Sit down, Beck," she insisted, while dusting off her pale, white hands.

I sat down on a wooden stool near one of the large ovens.

"Are you hungry?" she asked.

"Starving," I answered, having had only prison food for the past two days. Of course, it was actually pretty good stuff. Sheriff Pax's wife had made my meals. And even though it wasn't Millie-good, it was still tasty. I wasn't about to tell Millie that, however. Nothing made Millie happier than people enjoying her food. I figured I would have to eat my way out of this mess. "I've dreamed of your food for days."

Millie humffed and walked over to the far counter. She retrieved a round platter and placed it in front of me.

The platter held nothing but a couple of hard rolls and three slices of warm spongy cheese. It was obvious Millie was mad. The kicker was when she went to the sink and drew me a glass of tap water. Thomas left the room, looking like someone who desperately wanted to get away from what was coming.

I looked at Millie's stern face and figured I'd better just jump right into it.

"It was an accident," I pleaded. "I told you that. I never meant for those buses to roll into the lake. I didn't even want to go to the museum. If I had had my way we would have stayed at the school and watched a movie or played baseball."

"I'm sure if they had done that, you would have blown up the projector and given someone a concussion with a baseball," Millie tsked.

I was stunned into silence at Millie's tone. It wasn't like her to so blatantly point out my flaws.

"You can't blame what happened on the trip to the museum," Millie said.

"I can try," I pointed out. "I didn't ask those mushrooms to grow."

Millie reached out as if she were going to strike me. Instead, she stretched past me and pulled on one of the ropes on the wall. The tug caused bells to go off in other parts of the manor. Within thirty seconds, Thomas was back. Right behind him was Wane, and behind her was the groundskeeper Scott. All three of them looked like guests who had been invited to a fingernail-pulling party. They, along with Millie, grabbed stools and circled me. I spun around looking at all of them quickly. I felt like a spinning bottle and stopped with my eyes landing on Wane. It was my hope that maybe she would be a kind face to look at.

She frowned, and my hopes were dashed.

Wane was the youngest and by far the most modern person employed by my father at the moment. She had short dark hair and was pretty in a sort of smart-artsy-girl way. She usually wore light, fitted shirts and a half smile that was both ironic and sincere. In the past, the Pillage Manor had employed a staff of hundreds of people. But as my father had become more and more withdrawn and as he had self-exiled himself to the top floor, the staff had dwindled. Millie and Thomas had let almost everyone go. They had also sold a lot of the furniture and artwork to pay the taxes and keep the manor afloat. It wasn't until my father had been temporarily shaken from his madness that Millie and Thomas had been told that there was plenty of money hidden away in the Pillage family—enough to help repair the town after the attack, repair the damage I had done to the garage, and now pay for three school buses.

"This is uncomfortable for all of us," Wane said.

"Can I explain?" I pleaded.

They all nodded, and I told them everything about the past few days and how I had managed to end up in the lake with the buses. I used my best expressions and widest eyes. I tried to look contrite and humble, but I could tell by the way Wane was shaking her head that she wasn't completely buying it. I tried to really blame it on the mushrooms and work up some tears for a strong finale, but I just couldn't get my tear ducts to cooperate—I just wasn't a crier. The best I could conjure up was a couple of weak sniffles.

After I had said my piece, I hung my head and waited for them to swarm in around me. I figured they would wrap their arms around me and tell me how they had misjudged me and then beg me to forgive them for being so cruel. No one swarmed in. Thomas did speak, and his sympathy sounded like this: "Do you realize what you've done?"

I looked up.

"Do you?" Thomas asked quietly. His deep, still voice seemed to make my bones vibrate as a wave of sticky guilt shivered up and down my body.

"I'm sorry," I said lamely. "I can't help it."

"That's what we're afraid of," Thomas said dejectedly. "You're a Pillage and perhaps there's simply something in you that has a need for chaos."

"So it's the fault of my innards?" I asked.

"It seems as if the whole of you is born to act out," Scott spoke up. "You find trouble everywhere—like in the gardens, the conservatory, the basement, in society. You are a boy who needs less stimulation."

"I live with old people in an old manor in the mountains above an old town," I argued back. "I have no cell phone, no real TV, no Xbox, nothing stimulating at all."

"Still," Thomas said.

"Yeah," I said back, "*still* is all there is here. Endless stillness—it makes me miss the dragons."

Millie gasped.

"We need no talk of that," Thomas insisted. "Your family has carried that weight and burden for far too long. Let's not drag out old corpses just to get a look at them."

I had no idea what Thomas was saying. But I was tired, and tired of being talked at.

"I'm so sorry," I said contritely.

"Good," Millie said, followed by a deep sniff.

"You'll be required to stay in the manor unless escorted by one of us," Wane said.

"What?" I asked, dumbfounded.

"You are confined to the manor," Thomas explained. "You will be driven to school by me, picked up by me, and will abide in the manor unless one of us is with you."

"That's insane," I argued. "I can't . . ."

"You will," Scott chimed in. "We took you in and . . ."

"You took me in?" I interrupted. Something in the way Scott had spoken set me off. I mean, if Millie had said it I would have been all okay, but Scott had no right. He worked in the stables and hardly had anything to do with me. He was short in stature and wits, and his chin was covered with a wiry black beard. Scott had been the one who caught me trespassing in the back gardens at first. He was an expert at yelling at me whenever he felt I was doing things that I shouldn't be doing around the manor, so we didn't hang out much. On a couple of occasions

I had taken the time to help him weed some of the gardens and trim a couple of trees, but we had no deep relationship. Now he was acting like he was some trusted relative who had sacrificed all the love, money, and time he had to raise me.

"You didn't take me in," I shouted. "My dad pays you."

"Beck," Wane warned.

"What?" I snapped back. "In case you've forgotten, I was tricked into coming here. Remember? You sent for me."

"Don't let the child in you speak up," Millie tried to calm.

"This is crazy," I continued. "This was all an accident. Does my dad know what you're doing?"

"It is your father who has issued the decree," Thomas said sternly. "He will have you confined to the house and to the lower three floors until he returns from the hospital or feels you've earned a longer leash."

"Like a dog?" I said feeling the red in my neck rise to my face and color my whole head. "Chained up?"

"Beck," Millie said kindly, throwing out the first soft word in the conversation. "This is for your own good."

"Really?" I questioned, looking slowly at all of them. "I'm old enough to know that what you're really saying is that this is for *your* own good. Keep me locked up and your lives will be easier. Well, you can't . . ."

"Stop it, Beck," Millie interrupted, sounding like the mother of all mothers.

"I just think . . ."

"There's no debate," Thomas insisted.

I had had enough. I grabbed the little bit of food Millie had offered me and stormed off to my room. I had a lot to think about, and I wanted to do it somewhere where nobody but me could interrupt.

With all that had transpired, the family felt it was necessary to move to the Isle of Man in the middle of the Irish Sea. Edward quickly began to farm, but his bitterness made for poor crops. It was soon decided

The beginning of section six of The Grim Knot

CHAPTER 10

There's a Place

BY THE WAY, JUST SO YOU KNOW, adults continually baffle me. I had changed quite a bit since I had arrived here in Kingsplot. I was taller and stronger and, according to Wane, even better looking. I had also learned to occasionally consider other people's feelings. I didn't always need to be so concerned about myself being happy that I forgot about everyone else. I was a little more honest, a tad wiser, and definitely more likely to think before I acted. Sure, there was the recent bus thing, but if you remember, it was actually the mushrooms' fault. I was trying to be better, but every adult I knew couldn't see that.

Now I was being grounded like a little kid.

I was angry about what my father was doing to me, but I was also relieved to be back in my own room. There was no bed softer than the one I had, and I loved the huge bathroom across the hall that only I used.

I entered my room and turned on the light. Someone had been in and made my bed since I was last here. The drapes on my window were pulled open, and a nice warm light flooded in over the chest of drawers and the upholstered chair in the corner. I looked out the window and down toward the stables. I checked the window to make sure it was locked, and then I turned and walked to my closet. I opened the door and looked around for anything that might be hiding. I didn't see any mold in my room, but just to be sure, I got down on my hands and knees and double-checked.

Everything was clean. I quickly changed out of the prison clothes into some cargo shorts and a slightly obnoxious purple polo shirt that Thomas had bought me on a recent trip to town.

I pulled out the copy of *The Grim Knot* from the bottom dresser drawer. I had read the worn little book so many times that I about had it memorized. At first I had seen no value in the book, but now I loved the notes and words my ancestors had jotted down. I had even added a few things myself on the last pages to update what had happened with the dragons while I had been here.

I set the book down and picked up the stuffed animal next to it. It was a stuffed koala that a reporter—a horrible person who had met an awful fate—had given me. But seeing how that wasn't the stuffed animal's fault, I had named and kept him.

I put Mr. Binkers back on the dresser and set the book next to him.

There was a knock at the door. I opened it to find Wane standing there with a tray of food.

"Millie feels bad," Wane said. "She couldn't let you go the rest of the day without something decent to eat."

I took the tray from Wane and set it on my bed.

"Thanks," I said begrudgingly. "It's going to be really boring confined to the manor."

"Sorry, Beck," Wane replied. "It's for the best."

"Can I finally get a TV or cell phone?" I begged. "I need something."

"Maybe it's time for a TV," Wane conceded. "But let's not say anything about it for a couple of days. Let things cool down just a bit. Read your dictionary."

The dictionary Wane was talking about was the copy she had given me when I moved here. She had given it to me so I could look up the meaning of her name. Since then, however, I had used it to make the things I said in my head more interesting. I had most recently looked up the word *zephyr* after I had heard Thomas use it.

The food Millie had delivered was so good I forgot to feel

bad. Mille had sent up half of a roasted chicken with an amazing red-colored glaze on it. There were three rolls that tasted like clouds made out of butter and some cooked carrots that were swimming in some sort of brown sugar sauce. A mug filled with milk and a piece of chocolate cake wrapped up in a paper wrapper finished the meal off.

"Wow," I whispered to myself, marveling at what Millie could do with food.

I took my tray down to Millie, thanked her for being a food wizard, and then turned around and hiked back up to my room. I grabbed Mr. Binkers and lay down on my bed. I knew it was childish of me to keep the stuffed animal around, but it made my room seem less formal.

There was another knock on my door.

"Come in," I hollered.

The door opened, and a flash of red slipped in. Beneath the red were two blue eyes that I was very happy to make contact with.

"Kate," I said happily as I lay on my bed with Mr. Binkers.

Kate smiled and her pink lips made the formal room appear beautiful. "I see you have your stuffed animal."

I tossed Mr. Binkers on the floor and stood up. "Prison's changed me," I joked.

I took Kate's hand and stood up.

"What are you doing here?" I asked.

"I sort of missed you," she replied. "Weird, huh?"

"Concerning," I admitted. "Just so you know, I'm confined to the manor."

"Millie told me," Kate said. "I thought we could go up to the dome."

I was all for that. We both walked quickly to the stairs. We climbed up to the fourth floor, walked across the large empty hall, and took the next set of stairs to the fifth floor. We spent even less time on the fifth floor and climbed quickly up the sixth and then seventh. We reached the trapdoor that led up into the copper dome on the top of the manor. The dome was where my father spent all his time when he was in the manor. Of course he had been in the hospital for so many weeks now that we had decided to claim the dome for ourselves.

We pushed open the trapdoor and climbed up into the dome room. There were windows all the way around the edges, making the space light and airy. In the center of the room was a tall square wall with two doors. One of the doors led to a thin hidden ladder that ran all the way down to the basement of the manor. We had found the ladder after my father had been using it to slip out of the dome and travel through tunnels to get to the cave we had raised Lizzy in.

In the dome room there was an old worn bed, a table, and

a telescope pointing out one of the windows. Three of the windows were open with the wind blowing carelessly in and out. On the floor there were thick furs and on the ceiling was a map of the world.

"I never get sick of the view," Kate whispered almost reverently as she looked out the windows.

"Thanks," I joked.

"You sound like Wyatt," Kate said.

Wyatt was our friend, but he had an annoying habit of talking about girls as if every one of them loved him and was desperate to be with him.

"No way," I said. "Wyatt would have said, 'you're welcome.'"

Kate was thinking of other things and didn't waste any effort to reply. I turned and looked out the windows toward the back of the manor. I could see miles of overgrown gardens and trees. In the far distance the black walls of the conservatory were visible. It seemed like four lifetimes since we had first raised dragons in there. The air and mist of Kingsplot seemed to make even my mind soft.

I kept turning and gazed out toward the mountains where the cave was where we found the train and hatched Lizzy. I could barely see the dark opening hidden among the contours and crags of the stony mountain. All around the mountains were thick forests that stretched on for hundreds of miles. I then turned the opposite direction and looked out and down into the Hagen Valley. Kingsplot was many miles down and away, but through the low clouds I could see some of Lake Mend and bits of steeples and road.

"There might not be a better view in the whole state," Kate said.

"I don't know," I debated. "The view from the back of a dragon is pretty hard to beat."

"Yeah," Kate agreed. "I'll miss that for the rest of my life."

"You know that the bus thing was an accident," I said, bringing up what we still hadn't talked about.

"I know," Kate said nodding her head. "I was there, remember?"

"Those mushrooms were disturbing," I added. "And while I was in jail, a cactus from the museum came by and tried to turn me into a pincushion."

"Millie told me you destroyed a cactus."

"It destroyed itself while trying to kill me."

"What does it all mean?" Kate said seriously. "I thought this stuff was supposed to stop when you got rid of the stone."

Kate and I walked back down the stairs. When we were crossing the fifth floor, we could hear water running somewhere in the distance.

"Did you leave the water on?" Kate asked.

"No," I answered. "I haven't been up here for weeks."

"Is Thomas or Wane around?"

"Maybe," I said shrugging. "But they usually don't come anywhere near the fifth floor when my father's not in the manor. I'm not even supposed to be up here."

We walked quietly across the big parlor on the fifth floor. The noise seemed to be coming from down the west wing. I led Kate to the end of the hall where there were two doors. I opened the first one and it was filled with old washing machines, stoves, and a huge iron boiler. I looked around, but the noise wasn't coming from there.

I closed the door and we walked to the last door in the wing. Both of us leaned our heads against the white painted wood door. I could faintly hear the water running behind it.

I reached out and knocked.

Nobody answered.

"Open it," Kate whispered.

"What if someone's in there?" I whispered back.

"Isn't that what we're trying to find out?"

Kate reached out and turned the doorknob. It felt good letting her go ahead of me. It spoke volumes about what a believer I was in guys and girls both experiencing equal amounts of potential horror. I didn't want her for a second to think that I thought girls were less capable of going through strange doors and getting mauled first.

Kate opened the door slowly, and the sound of running water was loud and clear. There were no lights on in the room so I bravely stuck my hand in and flipped on the light switch. Nothing happened. Kate and I stepped in anyway.

It was a very large bathroom with two sinks, a toilet in the corner, and a large claw-foot tub near the far wall. There was also a large lounging area with a tiny couch and a fancy end table. I suppose the lounge area was designed for whoever was taking the bath to be able to sit and wait for their water to fill. Big, ornately framed mirrors hung on the walls, and there was a chandelier in the shape of a tree hanging from the ceiling. There was another door between two windows on the largest wall. We could clearly see that the faucet of one of the sinks was on and running. The sink basin was shallow and filled with water that was now flowing over the side of the sink onto the white tiled floor.

Like a really lame superhero that performed really mediocre tasks, I jumped into action, leaping across the floor and turning the water off. I then unplugged the sink so the water in the basin could drain down.

"Wow," Kate said. "Nice leap."

"I felt the moment called for it," I replied.

The two of us looked around. Something about the room made me uneasy; it was like looking at a face with no nose, something was off. There was nobody in the bathroom besides us, but it felt like more was here than met the eye. Light from the windows made the room bright enough to see, but filled the corners with shadows. Kate opened the door between the windows, but it was just an empty closet with bare shelves and a musty smell that was very familiar in the manor.

"So is this the beginning of a mystery?" I asked excitedly.

"Yeah," Kate replied. "The mystery of why Thomas forgot to turn off the water after washing his hands."

"That gives me goose bumps," I said sarcastically while pretending to shiver. "But seriously, Thomas doesn't come up here."

"Then Wane," Kate suggested.

"Wane doesn't come up here."

"Maybe it was Scott."

"Scott doesn't wash his hands," I pointed out. "Besides he hardly ever even comes in the house."

"Maybe it's just a loose faucet," Kate said. "Sometimes the plumbing in old houses can do odd things. I'd have someone look at it. It could flood next time."

I looked down at the ground. Luckily we had caught the water in time to prevent any large amounts from building up on the floor. There was just a thin wet path that ran across the length of the bathroom.

"Well," Kate said, resigned. "I should probably go."

"Okay, then I'll leave you alone," I said, motioning to leave the bathroom.

"Don't be stupid," Kate said laughing. "I need to go home. You're grounded, and I have homework."

"Actually, I am grounded, but I also have homework," I said sadly.

We both turned around, and I flipped the light switch off. As we stepped back into the hall, something in my mind tumbled, and the thought I had been trying to think finally caught fire.

I knew what was wrong.

It has been said that the world is bereft of strangers, that strangers are merely friends we've yet to meet. The peddler that showed up at their door was no friend.

The beginning of section seven of The Grim Knot

CHAPTER 11

Wanna Know a Secret?

EVERY BIT OF MY BRAIN STARTED to flash, letting me know I was onto something. I grabbed Kate's elbow.

"Wait a second," I whispered excitedly. "How can there be a closet door between two windows? There's no space for the closet to go into."

"What?" Kate asked.

I turned around and walked back into the bathroom. I looked at the two windows and the single door between them. I opened the closet door and started inside. It was just a tall empty closet that seemed to jut out the side of the manor.

"That's not a big deal, Beck," Kate said. "They must have added the closet after they built the place."

"So it just sticks out the side of the manor?" I asked. "I've seen the outside of this place hundreds of times and I've never seen a closet sticking out of any part of the manor."

I ran to one of the windows and tried to get it open. Unfortunately, like so many of the windows in the manor, it was swollen shut from time and moisture, and it wouldn't budge. I pressed my face up against the glass, trying to see to the side where the back of the closet must be sticking out. I could see a large brick chimney running up the side of the manor. One of the many chimneys the manor had. I pulled back and shrugged.

"It's a chimney," I said. "They must have built the closet into part of an old chimney."

"Smart," Kate replied.

"Yeah, I guess," I agreed, still feeling as if something were off.

I went to the closet and opened it back up. It wasn't very big and there were five bare shelves with thick dust on them. As I was stepping away from the closet my right foot slipped just a bit. I looked down and saw traces of water that had come from the once-running sink. The water ran up to the front of the closet and stopped. I looked back at the sink and then over at the closet once more.

"What are you doing?" Kate asked.

"I'm not sure," I admitted. "How long do you think that sink was running?"

"Not that long," Kate replied. "We didn't hear it when we came up, and we weren't up here that long."

"Still," I said thinking. "Shouldn't there be more water on the floor?"

"Maybe," Kate answered.

"And look," I said, pointing. "The trail of the water runs right up to the closet and then just stops."

There were a lot of things I liked about Kate. She was beautiful, smart, and wickedly funny. Her face was one of my favorite things in the world to look at. I loved how she put me in my place, but still saw something about me worth liking. I loved how she talked, the way she stood, and every motion she made. All those things aside, however, my favorite trait she possessed was her ability to recognize when things were getting interesting and her willingness to jump headfirst into what lay ahead.

Before I could say anything else, Kate was on her knees looking closely at the floor near the closet. She ran her hand along the doorjamb.

"Anything?" I asked.

"Maybe," Kate said. "Turn the water back on."

I was great at taking orders I liked. I plugged the shallow sink and turned the water on. In less than a minute the basin was full and beginning to spill over the side and down onto the floor. Water slowly began to build and then seep across the tile floor toward the direction of the closet. When the water reached the base of the closet it disappeared.

"There's a crack," Kate said. "The water's just dripping down below the closet."

"It's built into an old chimney," I reminded her. "I mean, the whole house is leaky. It's probably just . . ."

"Look at this!" Kate interrupted as she reached into the closet and pressed her palms down against the floor. "It sort of moves."

"So it's poorly built," I reasoned, hoping it was more than that.

"Look," Kate said. "It's not actually connected to the front wall at all. There's a crack all the way around. Can you get the shelves out?"

I shut off the water and then reached over Kate's head and grabbed hold of one of the closet shelves. I wiggled it, and it popped up just a bit. I tilted the heavy shelf and pulled it out of the closet. Kate stood up and helped me lean the shelf against the toilet.

"Clear them all out," Kate said excitedly.

We lifted and worked out the other four shelves. Each shelf was about four feet deep and five feet wide. We stacked all five shelves next to the toilet and then stood back and looked at the empty closet. Kate and I pushed at each other, fighting to be the first person to step in. We both got into the closet and turned around a few times looking for a trapdoor or a false back. The ceiling of the closet was solid wood, and the floor was carpeted in a red felt-looking material.

"It's just a closet," I said, disappointed.

"I was hoping it led somewhere," Kate added.

I wasn't in the mood to give up that easily, so I took it upon myself to investigate further by jumping up and down. The entire closet rocked slightly. Kate steadied herself as I bumped against the doorjamb that ran around the door. With my right hand I could feel a slight bump about chest high on the inside doorjamb.

"Kate," I whispered. "What's this?"

We both touched the small bump and then simultaneously pulled our hands back in surprise.

"Is that a button?" Kate asked with excitement.

I looked up at the ceiling of the closet and then down to the floor.

"It's an elevator," I said reverently.

We both jumped out so that we could properly move around in excitement.

"Unbelievable," Kate cheered.

We closely examined the doorjamb on the outside of the closet but could find no button of any kind. We stepped back into the closet a little more cautiously this time. We turned around and looked out into the bathroom. We let our eyes rest on the small button on the inside of the closet. After a few moments of quiet reflection, Kate glanced up at me.

"Push it," she dared.

I wanted to. The only problem was that I had no idea what would happen when I did. There was only one single, worn, flat button. There were no arrows or numbers letting you know where we might end up. It looked like we were standing in an elevator, but maybe it was just a trap and the button would blow us up or cause the walls to close in and crush us. Besides, the manor was old; what if the button caused some old cable to release us and we dropped hundreds of feet to a painful death?

"Are you going to push it?" Kate asked.

"Heck, yeah."

I had never been very good at critical thinking. I jammed my right finger into the button. A metal gate dropped from the top of the door and almost sliced our toes off. I was going to yell for help but Kate pointed out that it was just a gate to keep us safe during the elevator ride.

"That's a good sign," Kate said. "Apparently whoever built this wanted the riders to be safe."

I grabbed hold of the metal screen and easily pulled it up

a few inches. It was clear that we could open and close it as we pleased. I let go of it, and it snapped closed again.

"Well, we're not moving," I said needlessly.

"Maybe you have to push the button twice," Kate suggested.

I reached out and did just that.

Once again I was acting out before I had properly thought things through.

Kate and I held onto each other and screamed as the elevator . . . did nothing. No drop, no movement, nothing.

Kate stopped screaming first.

Once I caught on that nothing had happened, we both looked at each other and laughed with embarrassment. I let go of Kate, feeling relieved that I hadn't actually hopped into her arms like a frightened woman. I was a man, but I wasn't too proud to use the height and arms of someone else to keep me from harm.

"Push it again," Kate said one more time.

I pushed the button a third time, then a fourth, and a fifth. Nothing happened. We looked for any other button or sign, but there was nothing.

"Maybe it's just a cage," I said.

Kate and I lifted the metal screen back up. It rolled up into the top of the door frame and clicked into place. Once it was in place you couldn't tell it was there.

"It's probably just broken," Kate said. "Or maybe it never worked."

"It has to work," I insisted.

"Just because you want it to doesn't mean it has to," Kate said with disappointment.

"Don't be such a wet blanket," I said, not fully understanding the saying myself. "Because wet blankets are cold and uncomfortable," I tried to explain.

"Right," Kate said. "That's why they say that."

"All I know is that they wouldn't put in an elevator just to look at," I debated. "There has to be a purpose to this thing."

"As much as I wish you were right, you might be wrong," Kate said. "Think about it. We found a train in a cave, dragons in the garden, and slides behind the walls. Some of it makes sense, but most of it just points clearly to the fact that your family is nuts. This might be the nuttiest thing of all—an elevator in a closet? This house has more stairs in it than any place I've ever seen. Why would they build an elevator and then hide it in a bathroom?"

"Maybe one of my relatives was like Batman," I suggested. "All secretive and stuff. They'd run in here, take the elevator down to a secret hideout, and then save the world."

"Your relatives might have run in here, but it was more likely to use the toilet than save the world."

"My heritage is offended," I told her.

"Your heritage has more to worry about than what I'm saying."

"That's true. So let's go look at the chimneys outside," I suggested. "And check the other floors beneath this to see if there are crazy closets and openings there."

"Okay, but I have to hurry," she said. "My parents will go crazy if I'm too late."

The two of us put the shelves back into place and closed the closet door. We then ran down to the next floor and found the bathroom directly beneath the one we had just been in. There was no closet. We checked the next three floors. Those two had no closets and no openings that connected to the shaft. We couldn't check the basement because it was filled with dirt.

"So there's an elevator that doesn't go anywhere?" Kate asked.

"It could go up," I suggested.

"But there's only two floors above it," Kate pointed out. "And it doesn't go to the dome because it's not in line with it."

"It could go to the basement," I reminded her. "There's just no way we can know for sure."

I held Kate's hand and led her outside and around the west end of the manor. Following the brick path, we made it to the side of the manor where the brick chimney that housed the elevator was. The chimney looked just like all the others on the manor. I could see three others on the west side alone. I never would have thought that there was an elevator inside any of them. The chimney ran from the ground all the way to the very top of the manor where it stuck up about ten feet above the seventh-floor balcony. We examined the part of the chimney shaft we could reach, but it was nothing but solid brick.

"Someday they're going to write books about this house," Kate said.

"We could go to the roof and check out the chimney from the top," I suggested.

"I have homework," Kate complained. "Tomorrow after school."

I agreed.

"Promise?" Kate asked, wanting reassurance. "Don't go exploring it without me. I want to be here when you figure this out."

"I promise," I replied.

I walked Kate down to the bottom floor and down our long driveway to the gate at the front of the property. I kissed her as the sunset waned and she slipped off like a star of her own. I had homework to do, but more important than that, I had a promise to break. Kate would understand.

I ran all the way back to the manor.

There are things much more worrisome than poverty and hardship. Sometimes hardship can be a welcome companion. Curses, on the other hand, are nothing but rot.

The beginning of section eight of The Grim Knot

CHAPTER 12

Please, Please Me

I WAS RUNNING BACK UP THE DRIVE when I heard Wane calling my name from the courtyard near the fountain. She didn't sound mad, so I decided to find out what she wanted. I dashed around the fountain and over to her. She was standing near the blue Mercedes with keys in her hand and a half smile on her face. It was the kind of face she made whenever she had news to deliver that she wasn't sure I would like.

I should have pretended to not hear her.

"There you are," she said. "Your father has asked me to bring you to see him."

I was torn.

I wanted to see my father, that wasn't what was tearing at me. I hadn't seen him for days, and even though he was sick and a bit confused lately, I loved him. Our visits were always short but important to me. The reason I was torn was because I knew I was in trouble. I had destroyed property and been incarcerated since we had last spoken, and whereas it might be fun to catch up, it would be painful to fill him in on those occurrences. My father was not a man to be trifled with, and I felt very much that I had been caught trifling.

I skidded to a stop five feet in front of Wane. "He wants to see me now?"

"Now," Wane said.

"It's kinda getting late," I said, looking at the slowly dimming sky. "Shouldn't we wait until tomorrow?"

"He's insisting that he see you now."

Wane opened the passenger-side car door, and I climbed in. She then got in her side and started up the car.

As we made the almost hour-long drive to the hospital, Wane lectured me and tried to teach me things—taking advantage of a captive audience like most adults do. By the time we reached the hospital, I felt so preached at that I thought it was Sunday.

The hospital was in a beautiful, old building near the west end of Kingsplot. The building was made out of wood and stucco, and I could see the top of the large glass atrium in the center of the roof.

Wane stopped the car in front of the hospital and instructed me to go in.

"I'll be waiting out here for you," she said.

"You're not coming in?"

"He wants to talk to you alone."

I shrugged and started to think of all the things I would never accomplish in my life, seeing as this would probably be my last free moment alive.

I walked in through the large wooden door and signed my name on a piece of paper near the front desk. A lady with a really big nose called an orderly, who promptly marched me to my father's room.

We turned down two different halls and walked through three sets of locked doors before we arrived at his room.

#19.

The orderly patted me on the back and informed me he would be waiting outside of the door for me if there were any problems.

I knocked firmly.

"Come in," my father's voice called.

Pushing open the door, I slipped in. As the door clicked closed behind me, I heard, "Beck."

I could see my dad sitting on a chair in the corner of the poorly lit room. He was wearing a blue bathrobe and black slippers over white socks. His gray hair was a mess, and he had the makings of a pretty good beard. He was almost perfectly still; the only motion was his ring finger on his left hand tapping against the wooden arm on the orange chair. He looked at me, and I knew I was in for it. Even in his most troubled stages, he had always tried to not frighten me. Now, he looked like a ghost from *Scrooge* who had come not only to haunt, but to hurt me.

"Sit," he said calmly, never taking his eyes off me. I sat down on the edge of his bed.

"You look good," I tried.

My father grunted.

"I got a B on my math test," I said, throwing out the one good thing I had done in the last few days.

"Math's important," he replied.

"The mountains are really green," I tried. "It's like they know summer's coming."

"Beck, I didn't ask you to come so we could talk about the landscape," he said briskly.

"Right," I waved. "You just wanted to hang out with your only child—a little father-son time. I understand. I probably should have brought a ball and mitt so we could play catch."

I wasn't trying to be sarcastic, but the feeling in the room was grim. It was as if we had gathered to talk about the death of someone we loved dearly. I could see the pain in my dad's eyes, and I knew I needed to do something. I had messed up. I had made a mistake and cost him more money all while he was still in the hospital fighting to get well. I was making his life worse, not better. I figured I needed to just come out with it, take my lumps, and then spend the rest of my days working to repair what I had done.

"Listen, Dad," I began. "I know I messed up really bad. I'm sorry. I didn't mean for any of it to happen. It's not like I went to the field trip thinking, 'How can I ruin as many things as possible?'"

My dad kept quiet, silently soaking in my sincere confession.

"Trouble just seems to find me," I continued. "Every plant in the area wants to mess me up constantly. I can't go anywhere. And now I'm grounded. Trust me, if I could do it all over I would have faked sick and just not gone on the field trip."

It might not have been the wisest thing to say, but it was honest. I had said my piece, and now it was time to just sit still and appear remorseful.

My father looked at me and closed his eyes. He opened them back up, and his head bobbled slightly. I could feel the tongue-lashing that was about to happen. I held my hand up in front of my face, as if he were literally about to dump painful words down on me.

"Beck, you must plant that stone," he whispered fearlessly.

I put my hand down and looked around. "What?" I asked, not believing for a moment what I was hearing.

"The stone," he said urgently. "You must plant it."

"I can't . . ."

"You don't understand," he interrupted. "You must. None of this will change until that last stone is planted and what needs to happen is finished."

"Dad, you can't be . . ."

"My mind is slipping," he said. "The darkness our ancestors have been suffering from since Edward will kill me. There's only one way, Beck. Where is the stone?"

"Gone," I said.

"That's a lie!" he hollered. "You would never destroy it, you're a Pillage."

I scooted over on the bed, not liking the way this conversation was going. The words my father was saying scared me not only for him, but for me. I already knew that I was not above the illness affecting him.

"Where is it?" he asked again.

"I got rid of it," I insisted.

"Find it, Beck," my father pleaded. "Please, I can't fight off these dark feelings much longer. You must find it. You must save me. My life is in your hands."

"You said I should never trust my hands," I reminded him.

"Beck, I'll perish."

I looked around at the dark but comfortable room he was now in. "The doctors are saving you, Dad. It's just going to take some time."

"I don't have much time," he said, trembling. "Neither do you."

"What's that mean?" I asked defensively. "What do you mean I don't have time?"

"It's coming to get you," my father said slowly, while standing up. "It knows you're out there, and it will wrap itself around your mind until you do as it wishes."

"I don't understand," I said nervously. "Who?"

"The same madness that I hid from for years," my father continued, not sounding like the person I knew he was. "The reason I locked myself up in the top of the manor. The reason every woman in our family has gone mad and every man has died. We did this. It began with Edward, and it has to end with us. You can pretend you are fine, Beck. You can wait it out like I tried to do, but someday soon it will descend upon you like a personal plague. It will wrap its arms around you and smother you until all you love are dead."

I stood up and backed away from my dad. He was not well. It made my heart feel like a pressure point that someone was pinching with pliers. This was way too heavy for me. My father had always been off, but now he was scaring the tar out of me. The sickness in his head was out of control and I knew from experience that he was capable of harming me.

"I should go," I said.

"Yes," my father said almost gleefully. "Go, plant the stone."

"I can't do that," I pleaded. "It's gone."

"Plant the stone!" my father demanded.

"Dad . . ."

My father reached out as if he were going to strike me, stopped himself, and then collapsed back into his chair in a heap of body and bathrobe. I looked down at him and felt nothing but pity and sadness. My family was crumbling. All the strides my father was making to get well had just been set back years.

"Go," my dad whispered with his head still buried in his own chest. "This darkness will grow until we are both destroyed, unless you plant that stone."

I thought about saying, "I love you," or, "See you later," but the mood didn't call for it. So I backed up and left silently. I walked out of the room, closed the door, and walked down the hall. I had to be buzzed through the locked doors, and when

I passed the front desk, the lady with the big nose didn't even look up.

Wane was outside with the car still running. I got in and pretended as if nothing were wrong. I had a lot to think about, and the last thing I wanted was Wane asking me endless questions about my father as we drove back to the manor.

"How is he?" she asked.

"Fine," I lied.

"Good," Wane said. "I think this place is helping."

"Looks that way," I replied.

"It's going to be so nice to have him better," Wane said softly. "He deserves to be happy."

"Yeah," I agreed, knowing what it would take to make that a possibility.

"Let's hope he gets well soon," she added.

I buckled my seat belt, leaned back, and began to think of how I was going to retrieve that final stone.

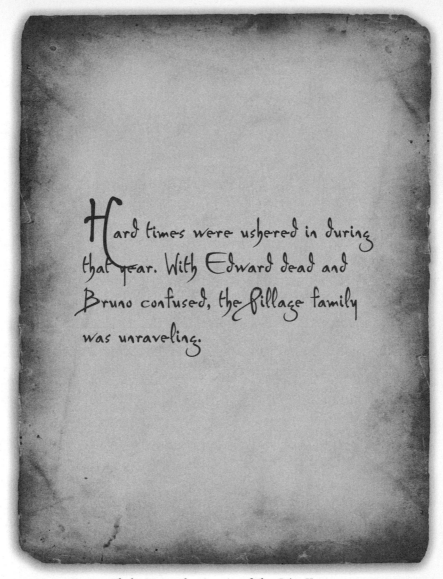

Hard times were ushered in during that year. With Edward dead and Bruno confused, the Pillage family was unraveling.

The beginning of section nine of The Grim Knot

CHAPTER 13

I Should Have Known Better

N O DREAMS FILLED MY HEAD and I slept remarkably well considering all the things I had happening in my life. It was sort of like my mind shut off and allowed me a good night's sleep in preparation for all that lay ahead.

After a breakfast of cinnamon rolls that would make even the Pope consider baked goods a sin, I tried to pretend that all was well with the house and just walk out the door to take the bus.

"Not so fast," Millie said, stopping me. "Thomas will take you."

"But . . ."

"Butts are for spanking," Millie said. "Now sit and wait for Thomas."

Thomas drove me to school and lectured me the entire time

about the importance of reputation and how it was my responsibility to bring the Pillage name "accolades and not atrocities."

I made a mental note to look up *accolades* in my dictionary when I got home. I had no idea what it meant, but I liked the sound of it.

Thomas pulled around to the back entrance of Callowbrow. He said something else about virtue and integrity, and I promised him I would do my best to round up some accolades for him. I then hopped out of the car and shut the door respectfully. I hadn't been back to school since the bus incident, and it suddenly felt too soon. I had the urge to not be anywhere near there at the moment. I turned to flag Thomas down and beg him to take me back home, but he was already gone.

Wyatt was standing by the back door talking to a girl who looked as if she were trying to get away from him. I stepped up and helped her out.

"Hey, Wyatt, can I talk to you?"

"I'm kinda busy," Wyatt replied.

"It's okay," the girl insisted, "I need to go." She looked at me as if I had done her a great favor and ran off.

"What the heck?" Wyatt asked. "I was just about to ask Ashley to prom."

"You should thank me, then," I said. "She was going to say no."

"That's not true," he said defensively.

"Actually," I corrected. "She was going to say, no way."

"Whatever," Wyatt said. "You're lucky you have Kate to take."

"Take where?" I asked, genuinely confused.

"Prom."

"I don't think we're going," I informed him. "Kate's not really into that kind of stuff. She's always making fun of proms."

"Your loss," Wyatt said. "There's going to be a ton of girls there."

I stared at Wyatt. "You know people don't go to prom to pick up girls, right? They take girls there."

"Well, maybe it's time someone shook things up."

I laughed at Wyatt and begged him to please stop being so stupid.

"Whatever," he said. "Why are you here early?"

"Thomas drove me," I told him as I reached out for the back door of the main hall. "I'm not only grounded, but I'm being driven wherever I go."

"Sucks to be you," he observed, stepping into the school with me.

The second we got into the building we were surrounded by chaos and confusion. Students, faculty, and even a few cops were running around talking and yelling loudly. All over the floor were long strands of crunchy yellow trash. I stopped a tall kid with a short neck to question him.

"What's going on here?" I asked.

"Someone broke into the school," the kid informed us. "They dumped garbage everywhere."

I looked closely at the floor. The yellow stuff wasn't garbage, it was . . .

"Uh-oh," I said mournfully as the no-neck kid walked off.

This was bad. I could tell that the odd garbage all over was long, dead stalks of dried corn. I had no idea how they had gotten here, but I had a feeling that it had something to do with me.

"What is it?" Wyatt asked.

"I've got to get out of here," I insisted. "Listen, if they . . ."

"Beck!" Principal Wales yelled from down the hallway. "Beck!"

It was too late. I looked at Principal Wales and thought about running, but I knew eventually I would get caught and things would only be worse. I stood up tall and swallowed like a guilty man in front of a smart jury. He stormed up to me with his stocky arms waving and his thick legs twitching madly. I decided to try a preemptive strike.

"I didn't do anything," I argued. "Nothing at all."

"Do anything of what?" Principal Wales demanded, his face red and his neck steaming like a warm sewer top.

"I have no idea," I said honestly. "But something must have happened here, and I didn't do it."

"Come with me," Principal Wales said, grabbing me by my right elbow. "I have something you should see."

He led me down the hall into the commons area. There were strands of dried cornstalks everywhere. There was a huge handmade banner on the wall with the prom theme, On the Wings of Love, painted on it.

"That's beautiful," I laughed.

We stomped across the crunchy yellow kernels and leaves and into the area where the upper-class lockers were.

"Do you recognize this hall?" he asked in a huff.

I was suddenly offended. It wasn't like I was dumb. I knew this hall. I was an upperclassman and my locker was in here.

"Of course," I replied, wondering what the heck was going on. "This is where my locker is."

Principal Wales walked me up to my locker and let me go. I stared at what used to be my locker. Now it was just a beaten-apart metal hole. The door had been ripped off, and my stuff was strewn all over. The ground was littered with fuzzy yellow strands, and the inside of my locker was covered with dried corn and leaves.

I let my jaw drop to show my surprise.

"Well," Principal Wales said, motioning toward my locker. "How do you explain this?"

I looked down both directions of the hall. No other locker had been picked on, and people were gathering to see what Principal Wales was going to do to me. Wyatt had followed us and was watching as if something exciting was about to happen.

"I'm not sure what I'm supposed to explain," I argued. "You brought me down this hall, asked if I recognized it, and then took me to a spot you know I've seen hundreds of times. Are you feeling okay?"

"Beck," he said, stamping his fat little feet. "Someone transports an entire field of dry corn into our school, and the only damage is to your locker. Don't you find that peculiar?"

"I'm outraged," I said. "I feel violated."

"This is not funny," Principal Wales pointed out. "Everything in life is not funny."

I kinda thought his big face spitting as he spoke was funny, but I had the good sense to keep it to myself.

"Let me tell you," he continued. "You've been nothing but a distraction and problem. Your family is a bunch of elitists; you blew up our shop shed, destroyed three of our buses, and now this. What can . . . ?"

Principal Wales continued to list all the many things I had done wrong since I had arrived. I wasn't surprised to hear I had done so many bad things; what surprised me was that with everything he was bringing up, he made no mention of the dragons I had unleashed on the town about a year ago. No mention of the dragons that had torn apart a lot of his school and wreaked havoc on the entire valley for an afternoon. It seemed as if he should have made some mention about dragons. Sheriff Pax was right about something being off here.

"And you still owe the lunch lady three dollars for those wieners you wasted," he finally concluded.

"I already told you I was doing an experiment," I defended myself. "Someone told me that if you throw a raw hot dog just right it will come back like a boomerang."

A few of the students around us laughed.

"Beck," Principal Wales raged. "Stop talking and look at this mess. Someone is responsible for this."

"Why would I break into my own locker?" I reasoned. "I should be the last person you suspect."

"Ha!" he exclaimed. "That's just your reasoning. You did it to throw us off."

"Throw you off from what?"

"From . . . you . . . our . . . the school is a mess!" Principal

Wales was so angry I thought his head was just going to rocket off of his shoulders and blast through the roof.

"I had nothing to do with this," I reiterated.

"I don't care," he said. "Those buses were expensive, and you are in need of some time away from here."

"I didn't do this."

"That is of no interest to me," he said, sniffing. "You are suspended for the next three weeks."

"But . . ."

"Butts are for sitting on," he seethed.

Adults have the worst sayings. I suddenly wanted to know where grown-ups came up with all the things they said, because most of them were awful.

"I promise I had nothing to do with this mess," I explained. "And whether you want to believe me or not, the bus thing was an accident. Besides, if you suspend me I'll just have more time to mess up."

"That's true," Wyatt said from the crowd.

Principal Wales glared at him, and Wyatt withered back into the crowd.

"So, is that a threat?" Principal Wales demanded, turning back to me. "Are you saying that if I suspend you, you'll cause more harm?"

"It's not a threat," I assured him. "It's just reality."

Principal Wales spotted someone coming down the hall and waved them over. I looked to see who it was that the crowd of students was letting through. I recognized the thin mustache and pained expression instantly.

"Sheriff," Principal Wales said. "If you could have one of your men escort this ruffian off the premises, it would be much appreciated."

Sheriff Pax shook his head sadly. "Of course."

"I didn't do this," I told him with spirit. "And I shouldn't be suspended for something I didn't do."

"That doesn't matter at the moment," Principal Wales said. "Let's pretend you're being suspended because of the buses."

Some people just can't forgive and forget.

"Come on, Beck," Sheriff Pax said kindly. "Let's get you home."

"Great," I said, throwing my hands up and knowing that I was now headed for another car ride and lecture.

"I want answers," Wales wailed. "I want to know why you did this."

As Sheriff Pax escorted me down the hall toward the front of the school, all the other students stared at me. I heard a boy I had never spoken to look at me and say, "It's about time."

The way he said it made it sound as if I were some notorious serial killer who had eluded the police for years. Other students pointed and laughed while I took the walk of shame. I wasn't too bothered until I saw Kate. She was just coming in through the front doors as we were going out. She looked amazing, and I . . . looked like a criminal. I waved while she shook her head. I tried to get Sheriff Pax to stop, but he nudged me forward.

"What happened?" Kate mouthed as I passed her.

"Call me," I mouthed back.

All the other students in front of the school were gaping and gawking at me.

"I'm innocent," I yelled, feeling like the moment called for it.

Sheriff Pax's car was parked right out front. He opened the back door and for the second time in the last few days I got into a cop car. I couldn't help thinking about Thomas and all the accolades I wasn't bringing to the family name at the moment.

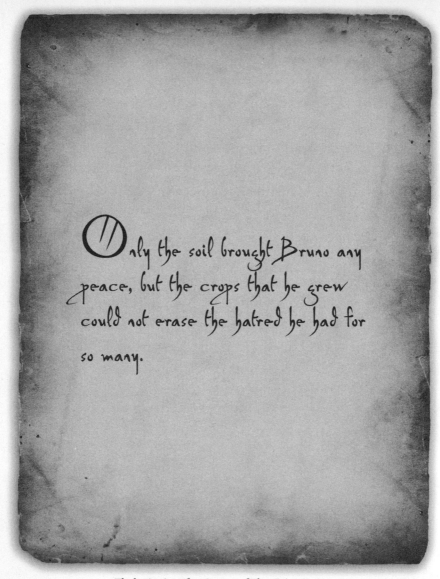

Only the soil brought Bruno any peace, but the crops that he grew could not erase the hatred he had for so many.

The beginning of section ten of The Grim Knot

CHAPTER 14

I Will

GOING SLOWLY, SHERIFF PAX PULLED out of the Callowbrow parking lot and drove two blocks down Main Street. He pulled over to the curb and turned off the car. We were nowhere near the police station and an hour away from the manor. I twisted my head. I couldn't see a donut shop or any other reason for him to have pulled over.

Sheriff Pax shifted in the front seat and turned to look at me through the metal screen.

"I didn't do that," I said, pointing back in the direction of the school.

"I don't care," Sheriff Pax said. "Do you remember what we talked about at the police station?"

"Maybe," I answered, not sure where he was going with this.

"I think something is happening in our town," Sheriff Pax

137

said with excitement. "Things have happened here that people forget—that I've forgotten—things about dragons."

"How have people forgotten?" I asked. "Dragons tore apart the town, remember? There are still buildings that aren't repaired. Look at that place." I pointed out the front window where a collapsed roof still had not been fully repaired. When the dragons had pillaged they had gone after anything metal or shiny, thinking there was value in it. In turn, they had torn off a number of awnings and lampposts from the street. I had noticed how so many things had been repaired, but it was almost as if the town had forgotten what ruined them in the first place.

"I can remember," Sheriff Pax said, confused. "But it seems more like an unimportant dream or a story someone told me."

"Do you remember coming to the manor and helping me rescue my father and the staff?"

Sheriff Pax rubbed his forehead vigorously. "Not clearly."

"Maybe you're just getting old," I suggested.

"It's not that," he said. "I can't get anyone else to clearly recall what happened. I have to write things down on my arms just to remind myself to keep investigating this each day."

"Weird."

"When I went to Callowbrow this morning, Principal Wales was having a fit over what had happened, but when

I questioned him about other odd things happening at his school he couldn't recall. Something's in the water."

"Or the soil," I said, surprised to hear the words coming out of my mouth. It was as if my soul wanted my ears to hear what it already knew.

"The soil," Sheriff Pax said to himself. "I don't know what to think about this."

I was really confused. Part of me wanted to spill my guts again to Sheriff Pax. The other part of me, however, wanted to just clam up and not say another word. I was already in trouble, and me saying more could only make things worse.

"What do you think happened at your school last night?" Sheriff Pax asked without malice.

"I'm not sure," I answered honestly. "Plants hate me."

"I don't want to sound bizarre," he said. "But it looks a lot like an entire farm of corn took over your school and broke open your locker. Like they were looking for something."

"Corn," I waved. "It's a weird vegetable."

"Beck, you know something more," Sheriff Pax pleaded. "Mushrooms, salads, stories of plants attacking you when you were in the hospital?"

"It sounds like somebody's remembering things," I said.

"Nobody remembers until I ask the right questions," the

sheriff said. "Even after they tell me, it doesn't seem as if they believe it."

"I need to get home," I said.

"Please, Beck, I need to know."

Sheriff Pax's voice was so unsteady and unsure. He sounded like a friend who was in trouble and needed help. Still, I had already told him enough.

"Do I need to call Thomas?" I asked. "I'm sure he's not even back home yet."

"I'll take you," Sheriff Pax said.

He tried to ask me more questions as we drove, but I kept quiet. So he changed up his plan and lightly lectured me. It was the second worst car ride I had experienced today.

Millie wasn't exactly happy that I had been suspended, but since there was nothing she could do about it, she fed me a small lunch and then sent me to my room to think about what I had done. When I told her I hadn't done it, she insisted I stop being so smart and just take it like a man. I guess men were constantly having to lie to make others believe what they thought was true, was true.

Life's weird at times.

It was hard for me not to cheer when I got back to my room. I was full, and I was free from school for three weeks. I needed to remember to act disappointed, but in my heart I was pretty excited to be home. I wouldn't be able to see Kate as much, but she could still visit me in the afternoons. Besides, there wasn't much school left in the year anyhow. I'd have only a couple of weeks left after my exile.

The best part of all of this was that I was now free to accomplish some of the things I needed to finish around the manor—two things I had written down on my personal to do list: 1) Fix elevator, and 2) find the stone.

Yep, I had already decided after coming home last night that I was going to get the stone back. I didn't know if I'd be able to find it, but I was going to try. The thought scared me, but I knew that it had to be done. I also wanted to find a way to get the elevator working. The biggest deterrents to being able to accomplish either of those things were Thomas, Millie, and Wane. I wasn't that worried about Scott. He stayed in the stables or outdoors most of the time. Thomas usually kept to the garage or one of the offices on the first floor in the east wing. So he wasn't a big concern. Millie kept to the main kitchen and her room in the east wing. Wane was the wild card. Usually she kept to the first floor or the gardens, but occasionally she would just show up at my room or come looking for me. And since I was grounded, I was worried she might come looking for me more than usual.

I decided to start with the stone.

I figured since the elevator was on the fifth floor, I could work on that at night and nobody would hear me. The utility room where the chute was located was on the first floor. And even though it wasn't too close to where people usually were, I knew it would be tricky.

"Let's do this," I said, trying to psych myself up.

I climbed down to the first floor and took the back hallway behind the main kitchen. I walked softly to the unused utility room in the corner of the east wing. I opened the heavy wood door and slipped inside. With the door closed, I turned the latch to lock myself in.

I walked between the old boilers and water heaters, past the dusty furnace, and down the two steps that led to the lower part of the room. Old tools and broken furniture in need of repair lined the walls, gathering dust and being forgotten by all who lived here. This utility room was never used anymore. Since there was no need to heat parts of the manor where nobody lived, there was no real need to keep all the utilities and guts of the manor in good repair. The main utility room was clean and functioning, but this was a forgotten space that nobody but a curious adolescent would ever visit.

I pushed through some old, folded drop cloths and boxes. There against the wall was the mouth of the chute I had previously dropped the stone down. I unhooked the hinge and opened the front of it. As expected, it was dark and quiet. I leaned my head into the chute and looked down—nothing but darkness. I whispered, and my voice echoed softly off the sides of the metal shaft.

I had no idea how to retrieve the stone. I was hoping to just open the chute and it would be there. It wasn't. I gathered some rope from one of the metal shelves in the room. I tied one end to one of the old boilers and then flung the rest of the rope down the chute. I heard it unravel and then grow silent. Now I just needed to clamber into the opening and climb down.

I looked into the chute and questioned my sanity.

I had no idea how deep the chute ran. It could go all the way to China for all I knew. There might be some Chinese citizen currently using the stone for a paperweight. I crawled up to the opening of the chute. I stuck my right leg in and then folded my left in as well. My feet were slipping against the metal sides. I crawled back out and took off my shoes and socks. I then climbed back in. My feet were able to cling to the sides of the chute, allowing me to shimmy down a few inches. I held onto the rope trying to muster up the courage to go down a bit farther.

I couldn't do it.

I needed someone to dare me. I was really good at doing dumb things when others were cheering me on. Striking out alone wasn't as easy for me. Sure, I had made plenty of mistakes by myself, but I was just better when I had an audience.

I crawled out of the chute and looked around for a flashlight. There were three in an old metal toolbox but none of them worked. I left the room and found two working flashlights in the laundry room on the other end of the hall. I took the flashlights back, shoved one in my right pocket, and flipped the other one on. I put the end of it in my mouth and bit down to hold it. I then climbed back into the chute. With a foot on each side of the chute, I slowly moved down a foot. I was only a few inches below the actual opening and already my legs were burning. I held onto the bottom edge of the chute opening with my right hand and took the flashlight out of my mouth with my left. I directed the beam of light downward, trying to get a look at what was below me. The beam of light was pretty strong, but it didn't reach far enough to light up the bottom. I dropped the flashlight and watched it fall forever. Eventually it snapped out. I didn't know if it had just fallen so far I couldn't see it any longer, or if it had hit the bottom and broken. Either way, there was no possible way I was going to make it down there like this. The rope wasn't long enough, and even if I did make it down, I could never climb the rope back up.

I pulled myself out of the chute again. I had thrown the stone down there knowing it would be impossible to retrieve.

Now that I had proven that point, I was pretty discouraged. My father would get sicker, then I would get sicker, and eventually my entire family would perish under the disease of dragons and madness. Our gift of growing things would die with me. A thought struck me.

"I wonder," I said aloud.

I put my shoes back on and ran out to the back of the manor. I looked around to see if I could spot Scott or anybody else that would complicate things. I walked along the brick path that wound through a maze of roses and over to the stone fence on the side of the manor. Near the base of the wall was a series of small clay pots with pansies and marigolds growing in them. I picked up a small pot and tipped it upside down, dumping out the flowers. I scooped up most of the dirt and took the pot to the wall, where I got down on my knee and dug in the ground beneath some strong ivy that was growing up the wall. I dug out a big piece of ivy and shoved the roots into the pot. I pulled the top part of the ivy off of the wall and bunched it up on top of the pot.

I looked around once more—still no Scott.

I got back to the unused utility room and locked myself in. I held the potted ivy near the opening of the chute and stared at it.

"Listen," I whispered. "You plants have been giving me grief for a while now. If you want me to plant that stone, you have to help."

The plant didn't say a thing.

"Fine," I said. "Be that way."

I heaved the pot filled with ivy down the chute. I heard it scrape and bang for a long while before it grew silent. I waited a few more minutes and then leaned my head into the chute and looked down. Then, like I had once done at the conservatory, I simply asked the ivy to . . .

"Grow!"

I put my hand to my ear, but I couldn't hear anything. I stuck my head back in the mouth of the chute and looked down into the darkness.

"Grow!" I hollered again.

The word bounced off the metal sides. My hope had been for the ivy to reach the bottom in good enough shape to still be alive. Then if nature really was so determined to help me out, the ivy would grow up the chute and I could climb down, using it as a leafy ladder.

I pulled my head out and groaned. I was glad I hadn't tried this with Kate. It would be right about now that she would point out how illogical the idea was.

I was standing there silently wondering if it would be possible to fill the shaft with water and then swim down to the stone when I heard something. At first it was faint, but then it sounded like a bowl of rice cereal popping and cracking.

Something was rising up from the chute.

I clapped with excitement and put my head back in the opening. As I looked, large ropes of ivy sprang out and shot across the room. The green strands wrapped themselves around the boilers and exposed pipes. In an instant the dusty old room looked much greener.

"Nice," I said, talking to the ivy. "I knew you could do it."

The ivy had come out of the chute on all four sides of the opening, creating a new green chute that I was hoping ran all the way down to the bottom. I climbed easily into the leafy opening and found hundreds of foot- and handholds to cling to.

"Much better."

I began the descent. Climbing down was a breeze—all four sides of the chute were like leafy green Velcro. My feet and hands flew down as easily as using a ladder with extra rungs. It wasn't long before the light coming out of the opening was at least four floors above me. I had no idea where this chute went or what its purpose was, but I was beginning to get a bit leery. I wasn't really scared of there being any monsters or people down there, but the possibility of spiders or roaches seemed almost worse.

I stopped my descent to pull out my second flashlight from my pocket. I flipped it on and marveled at the ivy cocoon I was in. I could have let go of the sides completely and not fallen more than a few inches due to all the growth. I suddenly wished I lived on the Isle of Man in the middle of the Irish Sea like my ancestors had. I wished I could farm and grow things that didn't ultimately destroy towns and families.

I kept going down.

It was warm now; the ivy and depth made the chute feel humid. I could see only a pinpoint of light above where the opening was. The thought of having to climb up was a little daunting, but I put it out of my mind and continued to descend.

"This is crazy," I said as I climbed down. "I'm going to end up in China."

I could no longer see any light above, and my mind was beginning to play tricks on me. For a moment I couldn't tell if I was going up or down. The ivy shivered, and I thought it was going to wither and die and leave me down here to do the same.

I was just about to give up and begin climbing back out when my right foot hit the bottom. I stretched down and felt around with my left foot. The bottom wasn't even, and when I shined my light at it, I could see that the ivy growing out of the dirt was surrounded by shattered pieces of the clay pot.

The chute actually curved a bit and headed sideways in a

different direction. I couldn't see the stone or any of the other things I had thrown down.

It was too small of a space to kneel down, so I scooted my legs into where the chute was running sideways. I then sat on the pile of dirt and pot and reached into the curve of the shaft to see if I could feel anything. My hand touched something plastic and I pulled out the flashlight I had thrown down earlier. The front of it was shattered, and the case was cracked. I set it down and felt farther into the chute.

I could feel the stone.

The moment I touched it, a small charge of electricity shot through my arms and made my entire body shiver. I reached farther and wrapped my fingers around it. I pulled it out of the chute and into my lap.

My brain and heart began to send pulses of excitement and exhilaration to each other. I suddenly couldn't remember why I had ever tossed this down here. This stone belonged to me. It would be a perversion of thought to not plant it and let it bring forth what it needed to. What kind of farmer doesn't plant all his seeds?

I heard a strange, almost maniacal laughing and realized it was me.

"Whoa," I whispered. "I might need help."

I pulled myself up and back onto my feet. I shoved the

stone into the right front pocket of my jeans. It was too large to fit all the way in, but it was in enough to allow me to make the trip back up the shaft. I turned off my flashlight and put it in my other pocket. I then began to climb.

I don't know if it was the joy of having the stone back, or the odd excitement of the moment, but something made the climb up faster than the one down. The ivy was so easy to hold onto, and in no time at all I could see the pinhole of light up ahead. I pushed myself, climbing as fast as I could. Soon the light was brighter, and I began to reach as high as I could for every hold, pulling myself up at a terrific clip.

When I reached the opening, I allowed myself to laugh again. This time, however, it was a little less maniacal. I crawled out of the chute and fell onto the floor. I grabbed the stone out of my pocket and looked at it in awe.

"Why did I ever let you go?" I questioned.

Of course if Kate were here, I would have had someone reminding me exactly why. But Kate wasn't here, and the stone and I were reunited. Now I simply needed the right place to plant it. I wasn't worried. It seemed as if the whole of nature was out to help me, and, to be quite honest, I was too hopped up on stone magic to recognize that just maybe it was helping me to my demise.

Naomi recognized the changes and dark moods of Bruno. It was her suggestion and push that caused him to finally plant the stone. As his aunt, she had always spoken her mind.

The beginning of section eleven of The Grim Knot

CHAPTER 15

Slow Down

S O, I SPENT THE REST OF THE afternoon in my room staring at the rock and trying to figure out what to do next. I now needed a place to plant the stone. I considered the conservatory in the back gardens, but Scott was a problem, and even though people didn't come around anymore to snoop and check things out, there was still the possibility of strangers finding it. I could have taken the stone back up to the cave, but there was no food there to feed the dragon, and it was such a journey to get there each time. I wanted to find a place with fewer stairs to climb.

There was a knock at my door. I took the stone and pushed it under my bed.

"Come in."

Kate entered.

I had lost track of the time, so seeing her was a surprise. It was much later in the afternoon than I had realized.

Kate gave me a pile of homework that my teachers had put together for me to work on while in exile. She then filled me in on the day at Callowbrow. According to her, most of the students had been forced to help with the cleanup of the rogue corn. She also warned me about how everyone thought the mess was my fault and how they all now wanted to personally show me how ungrateful they were.

"I didn't do it," I reassured her. "You told everyone that, right?"

Kate just stared at me.

"So you didn't defend my honor?" I asked halfway joking.

"I might have," Kate said. "But I wasn't completely sure you didn't do it."

"You think I snuck down there last night and broke into my own locker?"

"You do forget your combination a lot."

She was right about that.

"If it wasn't you, then who?" Kate asked.

"You saw all the corn," I reminded her. "I don't know exactly what happened, but I bet they were looking for the stone. The plants are restless. They want me to plant that stone."

"Well, I'm glad you didn't decide to hide it in your locker,"

Kate said. "The last thing we need is the danger that stone would bring if you planted it."

"Right," I laughed nervously. "I mean that would be terrible—or would it?" I asked casually, trying to test the water and see if there was any part of her that wanted me to plant it.

Kate stared at me again. "It would be terrible. Do you remember how close we came to dying last time?"

"Vaguely," I joked.

"You've ended it," Kate reminded me. "You put to rest what your entire family never had the courage to do. That's impressive."

I was beginning to feel a little guilty, knowing the stone I had so valiantly gotten rid of was currently under my bed.

"Let's not talk about that," Kate said cheering up. "I can't stay long, but I want to see the elevator."

I sat there silently on my bed in thought. I wanted desperately to tell Kate about the stone. I wanted her to know what my father had said and for her to understand how important it was for me to have retrieved it. I needed her to help me figure out where to grow it and then help me raise the beast that came out. I wanted all that desperately, but I was too scared to say anything. I knew Kate had the power to talk me out of things, but I also knew that this was something that had to happen.

"Are you all right?" Kate asked me.

"Fine," I said, shaking my reflective mood off. "Let's go see the elevator."

There was a hidden staircase behind a false wall down the hall from my room. Kate and I had found it a few months ago. It was really thin and only went as high as the fifth floor, where it came out in a storage room. It was terribly narrow and dark, so we hadn't spent a lot of time using it. But since the elevator was on the fifth floor, it was perfect. We slid the false wall back, climbed the stairs, and came out three doors down from the bathroom where the elevator closet was.

"Wyatt wanted to ride the bus and come see you today," Kate said as we walked into the bathroom. "I told him you couldn't have visitors. I want to investigate this without him."

"So you lied to be alone with me?" I asked happily.

"Something like that," Kate replied.

We opened the closet door and took out the shelves. We stood in the closet and pressed the button once again. The metal gate dropped down. I pushed the button again, but nothing happened. We scoured every inch and part of the closet again, hoping that there was some clue to making this thing work.

"Maybe we should tear open the wall below this floor to see if we can find something that might help us figure this out?" I suggested.

"Yeah," Kate said. "Thomas and Wane will never discover that."

"I'm just saying," I said. "It's an elevator. There has to be some way to get it to run."

"Wait," Kate said, as if she had just thought of something. "Wouldn't an elevator need some sort of electricity to work?"

I looked at her and smiled. "Could it be that easy?"

"Maybe," Kate said, smiling back.

"The power for this floor is probably shut off," I told her. "But I know where the fuse box is."

"Nice," Kate said happily. "Lead the way."

My heart began to race. I felt like I did when I was playing a video game and I had just figured out a clue that had stumped me forever. The moment before I actually tried out my theory was always the best, because in that moment there was the possibility that I would soon be opening new doors and levels. Now we had a solid idea that just might bring the elevator to life. If it worked, it would take us to levels in the manor we might not have seen before.

My heart raced even faster.

I led Kate to the first floor and past the main kitchen. I could hear Millie stirring something. We moved slowly and carefully so as not to make our presence known. I lifted my finger to my lips and waved with my other hand, instructing Kate to follow.

Past the kitchen there was a large wooden door with a gold handle and chipped door frame. I turned the knob and pushed the door open. I could hear the faint sound of a clock ticking, and a fly was banging up against a far window, trying repeatedly to get out.

We closed the door behind us.

"The laundry room?" Kate asked quietly.

"Yes," I whispered. "Right over there."

On the wall near the window was a large flat metal box. I pulled the front of the metal box open. Before us were most of the switches and breakers that controlled the electricity in the manor.

"Do you know anything about electricity?" Kate asked.

"Not really," I admitted, looking closely at all the switches. "I know that one Ben guy invented it."

"You mean discovered," Kate said.

"Right, that's what I said."

We both silently began to study the large selection of switches and breakers. There was a number near most of the switches. On the back side of the metal door was a list to what the number corresponded with. I thought that would help us figure it out, but the penmanship was so fancy and the words were so covered in grime that I couldn't read most of them.

"Does that say bathroom?" Kate asked, pointing at a dirt-covered word.

"I think that says, 'Beaker's room.'"

"Who's Beaker?"

"I don't know," I said. "Maybe it does say bathroom. What's that word?"

"Mush?" Kate guessed.

"Really?" I said, laughing.

Kate stretched out the sleeve on her shirt and took hold of it with her fingers. She rubbed the list on the back side of the metal door, attempting to clean it up a bit. While she did that, I used my fingers to brush off and clean some of the dirt-covered numbers next to the switches.

"This is ridiculous," I complained. "Some of this dirt is probably hundreds of years old. I say we just flip all the switches on."

"You don't think Millie will notice that?" Kate asked. "Suddenly the manor is bright with light?"

"She's kinda old," I reasoned. "Maybe she'll just think she's having a stroke, or seeing a vision."

"It's a bad idea, Beck," Kate said, reminding me yet again of her power to point out things I should and shouldn't do.

"If that elevator works, I want a ride, and I'm not blowing our chances by alerting Millie and Thomas."

We spent a few more minutes cleaning the list and investigating the switches. Some of the words were a little easier to read, and we could see that the switches were broken up into sections. The first floor had the most switches, and then there was a grouping for each of the other floors. We deciphered what cluster of switches belonged to the fifth floor, but there was no clear indication of which one worked what.

"None of the fifth-floor switches are even on," Kate said needlessly.

"So we'll throw all those," I said. "Nobody will notice, there's no one on the fifth floor, remember?"

"Wait," Kate said breathlessly as she was cleaning. "Look at this word."

The word Kate was pointing to corresponded with a number on one of the fifth-floor switches. It was dirty, faded, and fancy, but I could make it out.

"E-closet," I read slowly. I stood back and thought for a second. "Like e-mail?"

"Seriously, if anyone needs to be at school learning and not home suspended, it's you," Kate said, slightly disgusted. "It has nothing to do with e-mail. It might mean east closet, but there are a lot of closets in the east wing of the fifth floor. I doubt they'd all have their own switch. It must mean elevator."

"That's too obvious," I argued. "So Thomas knows that there's an e-closet upstairs?"

"This thing is so covered in dirt, who could know anything?" Kate said, not caring about that. "And it might not even be that anyway."

"Let's flip it and find out."

"Okay," Kate agreed. "But we should wait until Millie's using the blender or something loud so that I can signal you to . . ."

I wasn't as patient as Kate. I reached out and flipped the switch. It made a solid snapping sound, but that was it.

"Sometimes it's better not to think so much," I told Kate.

"You should know," she replied.

We both stared at the flipped switch.

"Let's go see if it worked," I whispered.

I closed the metal box, and we left the room. We slipped past the kitchen and climbed our way back to the fifth floor. When we got to the bathroom, Kate reached in and flipped the switch. The bathroom still didn't light up.

"The switch didn't say e-bathroom," I pointed out. "It said e-closet."

We got back into the elevator and turned so that we were looking out into the dim bathroom.

We gasped in harmony.

It wasn't bright, but there was a faint glow coming from the button. Every hair on my body stood up and did the wave.

"That was it," Kate whispered almost reverently.

"You wanna push it?" I asked.

"More than anything," she replied.

Kate stuck out the pointer finger on her right hand and firmly pushed the button. The metal gate dropped down as the sound of something wheezing to life could be heard above the ceiling of the closet. Kate held onto me as I held onto her. There was the sound of clicking and then a small rocking motion.

"Do you . . ."

I didn't have time to finish my thought. It felt like the world had dropped out from under us. The elevator dropped about five inches and then caught itself. The whole thing groaned and continued to move slowly downward. We watched the bathroom floor rise, and in no time it was dark inside the elevator with the only light coming from the dim, glowing button. We could hear the cables and gears clicking and grinding as we descended. Other than that, the air seemed deathly still.

"This might be a bad idea," Kate said, the gravity of what we were actually doing sinking in. "What if it doesn't go back up?"

"At least we're together," I said, trying to keep things light.

"That's sort of comforting," Kate admitted.

The elevator was dropping slowly. I reached into my pocket and pulled out the small flashlight I had brought. I clicked it on and was surprised to see how happy Kate looked. We were blindly traveling into the bowels of the earth, and she was still smiling.

"I like you," I said honestly.

"I know you do," she replied. "But there's a good chance we could be in trouble."

I moved the beam of the flashlight and shined it out the metal gate. We could see the solid stone wall moving upward as we went down. As we passed the first floor there was a mark with the number one carved into the stone to indicate how far we had gone.

"We're almost to the basement," I reported.

"Do you think it stops there?"

"Why would it go deeper?"

I kept the light shining out the metal gate. I could see a mark in the stone indicating the basement. We dropped right past it.

"We're going deeper," I said as the gears continued to creak and moan.

There was another mark in the shaft—then another, and another.

"It's going to stop eventually, right?" I asked Kate as if she were an expert on secret elevators and how they operated.

"This is so scary," Kate admitted.

"Don't worry," I said calmly. "Elevators are actually the safest form of travel—even safer than walking."

Kate shook her head.

"What?" I asked. "I read that in a magazine."

"Did that magazine take into account elevators like this?"

"Probably not."

After another thirty seconds, we both began to wonder out loud about whether or not we should press the button again. Kate thought it might reverse the direction we were going and send us back up to safety. I was worried that it would stop the elevator and that it would never start back up. If that happened we'd be stuck here until we were dead.

I made the mistake of thinking about how deep we were and how closed in the walls were. It made me remarkably uncomfortable. Suddenly there wasn't enough air, and I thought I was going to suffocate or have an anxiety attack.

The elevator began to slow.

The cables and gears ground and squealed in a group effort to stop us softly. With the flashlight shining out the gate, we could see the elevator shaft open up as we came to a stop and the box settled. There were two clicks, and then everything was silent.

"We're here," I said casually. "This floor is sporting goods and appliances."

Kate ignored my joke and bent to grab the gate and lift it up. I helped as much as I could, while still holding the flashlight in my left hand. I shined the light out into the darkness, and Kate put her hand in mine. Together we stepped out of the elevator like two explorers taking the first step into unknown territory.

We were in some sort of small underground cavern. I waved the flashlight around, and everything sparkled. The walls were like mirrors, and there were thick, stubby crystals growing from the wall and ceiling. Even the dirt shimmered. When I shined the light down, the entire place lit up like a massive disco ball. Kate lifted her right hand to shield her eyes.

"Wow," she said loudly.

"Yeah," I commented. "All we need is some groovy music."

The cavern was breathtaking. It wasn't huge, but it was compact and colorful like a prism that had grown out of control. We walked around the entire space marveling at how gorgeous and otherworldly it looked. I touched the ground and could see that it was dirt, but it had grains of glasslike sand in

it. There were some big pieces of crystal lying on the ground.
Like a true gentleman, I picked one up and gave it to Kate.

"It's so heavy," she said in awe.

"Only the heaviest for my girl." The sentiment sounded
more romantic in my head.

"You have a way with words," Kate said kindly.

We walked around the room a couple of times, checking it
out. There were no other doors or openings or elevators for that
matter. Kate described it beautifully by saying, "It's like a glass
house in the belly of the earth."

One of the most surprising things to me about the space
was that it was so empty— there was no furniture or structures.

"Why would there be an elevator coming down here?" I
asked Kate.

"Why not?" she replied. "It's spectacular."

Kate was right, of course. I could understand why one of
my crazy ancestors might have believed it was a worthwhile en-
deavor to create a way down here. Me? I saw its potential in a
different way.

"Should we get in the elevator and see if we can get back
up?" I asked.

"Yes," Kate responded quickly. "It's hard to completely enjoy this place not knowing if we'll be able to get out."

We stepped back into the elevator and turned around to

face the glass cavern. Kate closed her eyes, and I reached out and pushed the glowing button. The metal gate dropped, and the box began to shake and then move upward.

I shined the light at Kate. She wiped her forehead to show her relief.

"Let's just hope it makes it all the way," I said.

The elevator made it up with no problem. When we were safely in the fifth-floor bathroom, we put the closet shelves back into the elevator and shut the closet door.

"We've got to find a purpose for that space," Kate insisted. "It's too incredible not to do something with it."

"I agree," I agreed, not having the heart to tell her that I already knew exactly what I was going to do with it and knowing it would break her heart if she knew.

Eventually the desire to pillage was too strong to fight. It was a dark day when the gift of growth became a perversion of nature. No one saw

The beginning of section twelve of The Grim Knot

CHAPTER 16

Carry That Weight

ONLY I COULD BE SO QUICK TO break a promise. As soon as Kate left, I started my plan in motion. I carefully hiked out of the manor and back behind the garage. I kept a close eye out for Scott or any other person who might wish to stop me.

Going behind the garage, I followed the train track that led to the mountain. Once I got to the mountain, I hiked up the horrible stone stairs to the cave where we had spent so much time with Lizzy. I wouldn't have minded hanging out for a few minutes, but I had things to do. I went back into the deep part of the cave and trimmed off a small piece of one of the plants that was growing there. I took that piece with me and returned to the manor.

By the time I got back to my room, it was dark. I grabbed

the stone, used the hidden stairs, and returned to the bathroom on the fifth floor. I took the shelves out and hid them in one of the empty bedrooms next to the bathroom. I had rounded up a dozen flashlights from the garage and stables. I figured I would need to always have one on hand. I put the flashlights in the tub to use as I needed. I took one of the flashlights and wrapped a wire hanger around it. I then hooked the flashlight to the top of the elevator so that I would have a light on all the time. It was perfect. All I had to do was reach up to flip it on or off.

I turned around in the elevator and closed the closet door so that if someone did come looking for me they wouldn't just see an open elevator shaft. I pushed the button, the metal gate dropped down, and the descent began.

My legs were still tired from the long hike and from climbing the hundreds of stairs to and from the cave, so I was pretty thankful for an elevator.

It was a long, steady ride down.

When I finally reached the glass cavern, I took the plant I had harvested from the cave and planted it in the center of the room.

I stood up, dusted off my hands, and commanded the plant to grow.

Instantly, the plant began to grow and fill out. In a few seconds it looked like a small bush. Seeing the plant grow made me happy. There was no way what I was doing was completely wrong if even the plants were cooperating.

"Perfect," I said to myself.

I pulled the stone out of my backpack and looked at it carefully. I knew all the danger and destruction it held, but the part of my brain that paid attention to stuff like that was turned off. All I could see was the glory and thrill of raising another dragon. I could envision the strength it would have and the pillaging power it would possess. Sure, I knew that what I really was supposed to do was grow the dragon and then destroy it, seeing as it was the only way to completely heal my family. Deep in my heart, however, I hoped it wouldn't come to that. It had taken everything I had to destroy the dragons I had grown before. I wanted this dragon to be different. I wanted this beast to be noble and good so that I'd be able to keep him around.

"And maybe oil will gush from my nose," I said, knowing how unlikely that would be.

I hefted the stone a few times, begged it to please produce a dragon that would bring calm and not calamity, and then stared at it closely.

"I shouldn't be doing this," I told myself.

I set the stone in the dirt near the plant. It sunk into the soil a couple of inches, acting as if it weighed a thousand pounds. The plant next to it shook and then shot out leafy shoots into the ground near the stone. The tangled stalks burrowed under the stone and then popped back up and began to wrap the rock up. The plant twisted over and under the rock until there was no sign of stone.

The soil around the plant seemed to relax and exhale—it was as if nature recognized that it finally had its stone. No more stalking me in museums. No more picking on me in the forest. No more attacks from cornstalks or destruction of school property. Nature and the Pillage gift had come together one final time. Now the future and fate of my family was in the hands of destiny.

"Kate's going to kill me," I whispered as I stared at the leafy stone. I picked up the flashlight and shined it around the glass cavern. Light bounced and bobbed like lasers all around me. "How about we keep this our little secret for a while," I called out.

There was no echo, no reply, and no peace of mind. I had done what I knew was inevitable, and there was no turning back.

I walked back into the elevator and pressed the button.

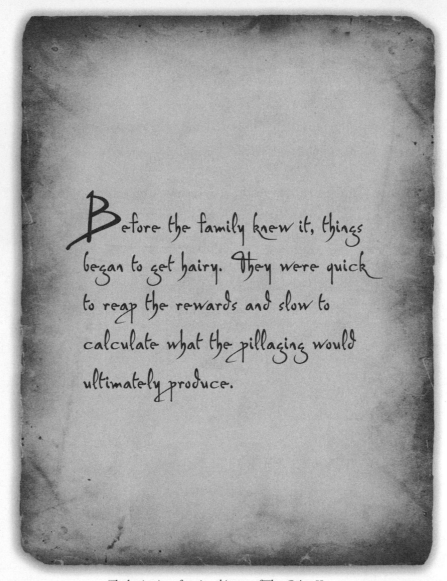

Before the family knew it, things began to get hairy. They were quick to reap the rewards and slow to calculate what the pillaging would ultimately produce.

The beginning of section thirteen of The Grim Knot

CHAPTER 17

Act Naturally

COMING TO GRIPS WITH WHAT I had done was remarkably easy for me. Since I had planted the stone, every day for the next week my schedule was pretty much the same. I got up, had breakfast, made sure Millie and Wane saw enough of me to ignore me for the rest of the day, and then headed straight to the elevator.

Each time I went down to the glass cavern, I would bring buckets of water and hay I had stolen from the stables. My plan was to little by little stock up on the food that the dragon would need once it hatched. The only way to get stuff down there was the elevator, and I couldn't take that much with me each trip. I also hauled a small portable gas generator and a couple of lamps down. The light helped immensely. When the lamps were on, the glass cavern was spectacular, and if I hadn't been actually standing in it, I don't think I would have believed it was real myself.

The plant around the last stone was growing thick and large, rapidly. It was now as big as a waterbed mattress and it hovered just above the dirt like all the pods had always done. The green closed nest made all sorts of odd noises and sounds, burping and gurgling like an impolite stream and making the room feel a bit like a simmering volcano.

The worst part about what I was doing was having to keep it a secret from Kate. She had come over every afternoon after school, and every time she was here she wanted to take the elevator down and explore the cavern. I had thought of a number of ways to explain what I was doing, but in the end I went with a lie that sounded like this.

"Someone turned the electricity off."

"Who?" she had asked.

"Probably Thomas," I replied. "And now he's asking me questions about closets. He knows something."

"So what should we do?"

I had told her we should lay low for a few weeks, not go anywhere near the elevator. Kate thought that was very responsible and grown-up of me. She also thought it showed great restraint. I thought it was more like rock-solid proof of what a horrible person and liar I was. Still, there was no way I was taking Kate down there. I had a feeling that when she saw the water and the hay and the lights and the generator and the growing nest that she might suspect I hadn't been completely up-front with her.

So Kate had no idea what was happening, and I tried to convince myself that keeping her in the dark was actually helping her. Unfortunately, as I was getting older, I was getting harder and harder to convince.

At the end of the week, Kate came over after school as usual. She spent some time with me down in the main hall helping me do some of the schoolwork I should have been doing during the day. She was an excellent tutor and made me wish I was bad at everything just so she could slowly explain it to me. I loved the way she talked in almost a whisper as if we were in a library instead of the manor.

"Do you understand?" she asked.

"I think so," I replied. "So Washington, DC, isn't in the state of Washington."

"Right," she smiled.

"You learn something new every day," I said happily.

"Of course, most people learn that on a day when they're in second grade," she pointed out.

"My childhood wasn't easy," I said defensively.

"That's it," she soothed sarcastically. "Blame your upbringing."

We moved from geography to geometry and then did a little Spanish. Kate was even prettier speaking a different language.

"What are you staring at?" she asked.

"You," I replied.

"Well, knock it off," she said nicely. "We're almost done."

"I can't help it," I replied. "It's your fault. You're really beautiful."

Kate actually blushed and started pretending she was looking for something in her backpack.

I closed my Spanish book and smiled at her coyly. "What say we knock off the books and go out into the garden?"

Kate looked at me with her blue eyes shining and her pink lips curled at the ends.

"I have a better idea," Kate said. "How about instead we turn the elevator back on and go down to the cavern?"

I tried not to let the panic show in my eyes or voice. "I don't think we should. Thomas was asking more questions this morning."

"About what?" she asked.

"Closets," I replied.

"So he just asks you random questions about closets?" she questioned. "What kind of questions?"

"Like do I think closets are important," I said, sounding like a fool and not being able to come up with anything else quickly.

"Really?" Kate said, tilting her head slightly. "And what did you say?"

"I told him yes," I lied. "I told him how I thought they made storing things really easy."

Kate was still just as beautiful as before, but I could tell from her eyes that she was growing suspicious.

"Tell me another question Thomas asked."

"They were all just closet related."

"One more," she pushed.

"Oh, he asked me if I knew the difference between a linen closet and a storage closet," I said sounding pathetic. I decided to add some Millie to soften things. "And Millie told Thomas to stop pestering me and let me eat."

"So you didn't answer him?" Kate said.

"No," I replied. "But for the record I would have said you put linen in linen closets and storage in storage closets."

Kate kinda smiled at me.

"Are you hiding something from me?"

"No," I said laughing. "Why would I make that up?"

"I can't stand it when people aren't honest with me," Kate said strongly. "You know that's my worst thing."

"I'm being honest," I lied.

"Something's not right," Kate insisted.

My palms started to sweat, and the soles of my feet

suddenly felt like they were burning. I knew from the popular saying that a liar's pants caught on fire, but I wasn't aware that feet could burst into flames as well. I figured that information was in a second verse that I had never learned, due to my poverty-stricken upbringing. Kate could smell blood in the water. She knew I was holding something back, and she was going to find out what it was.

"What's going on, Beck?" she asked sincerely.

I did the only thing I could. I stood up, knelt down, and then asked her to the prom. It was spontaneous, it was cheesy, and it was the only thing I could think up to take her mind off me and my lying. Kate was so surprised, she actually gasped.

"Prom?"

"It might be kinda lame, but it'll be a good memory," I explained. "I just think that . . ."

Kate interrupted me by throwing her arms around me and kissing me. I kissed her back, marveling at the fantastic direction our conversation was going. She pulled back and looked me in the eyes.

"So is that a yes?" I asked.

"Yes," she said with more joy than I had ever heard her express.

"What is it with girls and prom?" I asked her.

She was too excited to answer.

My mind raced with images of myself wearing a tux and having to open car doors and making reservations and having Thomas drive us and the lie I was hiding from Kate.

I should have felt happy. Instead I felt worried, and possessive of the secret I would never share with Kate.

"I should go," Kate said. "I need to tell my mom."

"Your mom hates me," I reminded her.

"She just doesn't know you," she said, standing up to leave.

"Chances are if she knew me she'd hate me more."

"That's a good point," Kate agreed. "Still, she'll be impressed you had the guts to ask me."

"What about your dad?"

Kate picked up her own backpack and slung it over her shoulder.

"I don't think I'll tell him just yet."

"Yeah," I agreed. "Wait until we're married and have a couple of kids."

Kate smiled, kissed me once more, and then left.

I felt awful. I knew the lie I was hiding was going to cause Kate big grief at some point. I sat there alone. My only hope was for the dragon to hatch, grow quickly, and devour me before it was ever discovered.

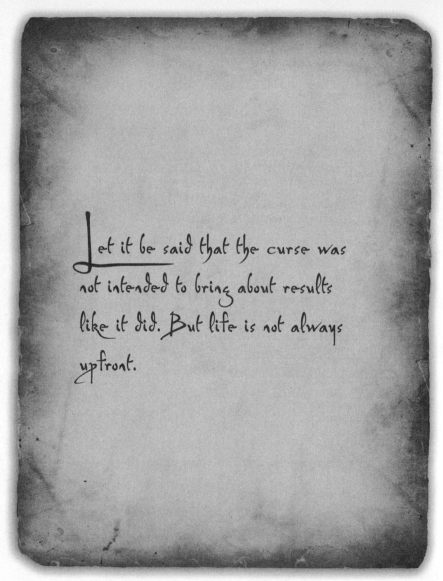

Let it be said that the curse was not intended to bring about results like it did. But life is not always upfront.

The beginning of section fourteen of The Grim Knot

CHAPTER 18

Any Time at All

LET ME SAY THAT I TRULY WISH I HAD learned my lesson while being suspended. It would have been nice if I had spent my days in misery and remorse wishing that I were back at school—but that wasn't the case at all. My days away from Callowbrow were going great. I spent all my time traveling up and down to the glass cavern. I was getting a pretty good supply of water and food ready for the day when the dragon hatched. I was even stockpiling containers of gas for the generator near the elevator. And one day I brought a wooden post down and installed it in the middle of the cavern. *The Grim Knot* had taught me long ago that dragons need some sort of post or pin to feel emotionally tethered to.

Kate still came over every afternoon. She still had some interest in the elevator, but her main concern was that I would be ready for prom. I guess she knew that sometimes I was a little loose with details and planning. I wanted to point out to her how well I was doing in my preparation for the dragon, but I knew that example would just complicate things.

On the second Friday of my life in exile Kate didn't come over because she had to complete some chores for her parents before the weekend. So I spent the evening assisting Millie in the kitchen and trying to be helpful around the manor. It felt good to be helpful, but it felt even better to go to sleep that night knowing that tomorrow was Saturday and the weather forecast was for warm and sunny. Nice days occurred so infrequently in the Hagen Valley that it was a big deal when they did. Millie had already promised me that I would be allowed to spend the day anywhere outside if it was sunny.

"It'll be good for you to spend some time outside of the manor" were her actual words.

I didn't have the heart to tell her that I had been sneaking out to gather hay and food for two weeks now. So I went to bed thinking the next time I was awake it would be sunny and warm.

At 2:15 in the morning, someone knocked on my bedroom door and it wasn't sunny or warm. I woke up and tried to figure out what was happening.

"Beck," Wane said through the door. "Beck, it's me."

"Come in," I mumbled.

Wane came in and flipped on the light. I blinked at the brightness and let my eyes adjust on Wane. She was wearing a sweatshirt and pants, and her hair looked like it could use a little care.

"What's going on?"

"Your dad," Wane said. "He wants to see you."

"But . . ."

"We tried buts," Wane said. "He won't wait until tomorrow. He wants to see you now."

It wasn't unusual for my dad to ask to see me at odd hours of the day and night, but unlike before when all I had to do was go up to the dome room, now I had to travel into Kingsplot, and someone had to take me.

"Put something on," Wane instructed. "I'll be down in the car waiting."

I was relieved that it would be Wane taking me and not Thomas. I like Thomas, but there was only so much time the two of us could spend together.

I put on a sweatshirt and jeans, used the bathroom, and then ran downstairs and got into the car.

"Are you sure you won't fall asleep while you're driving?" I asked Wane.

"I'm sure."

"Isn't this nuts?" I asked as we drove down the driveway.

"A little," Wane replied. "But it's the job."

Wane and Thomas and Millie seemed so much like family to me that sometimes I forgot they were actually employees of my father. They were paid to look after me and the manor.

"Still," I complained, "he could have waited until we were all awake. Is the hospital even open?"

"Visiting hours are long over," Wane said. "But your father still has some influence. The Pillage family has always been treated with exception."

"Do you know what my dad wants?" I asked.

"No idea," Wane said. "They just said he was frantic for you and needed you as soon as possible."

"Frantic?" I asked nervously. Most conversations with my dad were a bit awkward, but if he was frantic it would be much worse. "Last time I saw him it wasn't great."

"Your father is having a difficult time," Wane said. "The hospital is trying their best, but he's a difficult patient."

"And father," I said.

"And employer," Wane added.

The lady with the big nose was waiting in the lobby and opened the front door the moment we pulled up.

"She doesn't look too happy," I told Wane.

"Good luck," Wane said halfheartedly.

I entered the hospital and thanked the woman for missing out on her beauty sleep.

"It's what we medical professionals have to do sometimes," she replied.

It actually looked like she must do it a lot. I was escorted down the hall to my father's room. There was an orderly standing outside of his door. The orderly unlocked the door and motioned for me to go in.

My father was standing near the one window, staring at the curtains with his hands clasped behind his back. As the door snapped shut behind me, he spun around.

"Beck," he said, shaking.

"What's the deal, Dad?" I asked sincerely. "It's really late."

"That's of no consequence," he said, stepping up to me. He grabbed my shoulders. "Did you plant the stone?"

I nodded.

"Has it hatched?"

"Not yet," I reported.

"Tell me everything," he insisted, sitting down in the chair in the corner.

I told my dad everything. I told him about the elevator and how the nest was growing and the preparation I had been making. I told him about keeping it a secret from the rest of the staff so they wouldn't stop me.

After I had filled him in, my dad just stood there and shook. He looked like an aspen tree under the influence of a zephyr.

"Excellent," my father whispered.

"Thanks," I replied, not knowing what the proper thing to say was when someone complimented you on your deceptive dragon-rearing.

"Beck, you have to get me out of here," my dad insisted.

"What?" I asked. "I can't do that."

"Nonsense," he said. "I'm well. There's nothing wrong with me. You must get me to the manor."

My father's speech was suddenly awkward and stilted.

"I thought you said you weren't better yet," I reminded him.

"I never said that," my father snapped.

"You did," I argued. "You told me to plant the stone because you were sick and wouldn't get better unless I did."

"Well," my father said, looking confused, "you've planted it and all is well. Now get me out of here."

"Are you allowed to leave?" I asked.

"Yes," he lied. "They just won't listen to reason. There's a great need for me to return to the manor and they won't listen to reason. You'll tell them, right?"

"I can try," I said.

"I knew you would come through for me," my dad said,

springing out of his chair and rushing around the room. "We'll be back to the manor by sunrise. Who brought you?"

"Wane," I answered.

"We'll leave her here in town then."

"What?" I asked, confused. "Why can't we bring her back to the manor with us?"

"She'll be in harm's way," my dad said. "We'll have to release Thomas and Millie as well. Scott knows enough to stay. Besides, we might be able to use him."

"I don't understand," I said, beginning to feel a bit frantic myself. "Release Wane and Thomas and Millie?"

"Everything is about to change," my dad said excitedly. "Don't you see? I was a coward. For too long I have been fighting against what is rightfully mine—rightfully ours. I thought I was being valiant, but I was simply starving the real me."

I wanted to tell him that he was mad, but the words he was saying swirled around my brain and made me dozy. They felt warm and soothing.

"I—"

"Do you know what we have?" my dad asked. "Now with the soil under our control, when the dragon hatches, we will finally take what is rightfully ours."

"But . . ."

My dad packed up a few things and then marched to the

door. He knocked, and the orderly looked through the reverse peephole.

"Step away from the door," the orderly said through the intercom.

"Nonsense," my father said. "Let me out."

"We can't do that, Aeron," the orderly insisted. "Step back and we'll let your son out."

My father laughed and then spun around and ran toward me. I couldn't tell if I was in trouble or if my father was revving up to give me some sort of aggressive hug. He grabbed my right arm and twisted me around. He pulled my right arm back and put his left around my neck. He pulled me tightly against his chest as I faced away from him.

"Dad!"

My father shoved me forward to the door.

"Let me out!"

My dad had officially gone off his rocker. Memories of him disguised as Whitey and his willingness to let me die with Lizzy came washing over me like cold, dirty water.

The door swung open, and two large orderlies burst in. They both had big gloves on and looked like dog trainers getting ready to tussle with a ferocious beast.

"Let go of your son!" one of the orderlies commanded. "Release him!"

"No!" my father insisted. "Let me out and you can have him."

I looked at the mirror and saw the image of my father holding me captive. The room seemed to swirl and rock. I could see the darkness in my father's mind leaking from his eyes and nose. The Pillage scourge had completely taken him over. The madness that he had fought against was out in full force.

I tried to wriggle out from under my dad's arm. As I kicked and squirmed, one of the orderlies used the confusion to rush over and inject something into my father's right shoulder.

My father screamed, and the orderly wrapped his arms around my dad. I pulled free and fell to the floor.

"Let me be!" my father yelled. "You will be devoured."

"Out!" the other orderly yelled at me. "Out!"

I crawled frantically across the floor and out into the hallway. My father was screaming about dragons and tyranny and destruction.

There were four more orderlies in the hallway. One of them pulled me up onto my feet, while the other three rushed into the room.

"Are you okay, kid?" the orderly asked me.

"Fine, I think," I replied. "My dad's not so good."

"We'll take care of him," he said kindly.

"What's going to happen?"

"We'll have to move him," the orderly said. "We have some rooms that are a bit more secure."

My dad was still screaming, but now his words were slurred and incomprehensible. He made one last attempt to argue and then succumbed to the medication.

"You need to leave," an orderly said, taking me by the left elbow. "Come on."

When I got back to the car, it was beginning to turn light. Morning was starting to peek its head into the scenery.

I guess I looked disheveled because the second I got in, Wane said, "What happened to you?"

I filled Wane in on my father as we drove back home. I felt bad about my dad, but I was also surprised. There was something inside me that seemed pleased. With my father locked up, maybe I wouldn't have to share the dragon with anyone.

The thought made me feel powerful and momentarily happy.

I was so tired by the time I got back home that I could barely walk. Millie met us at the door and handed me a glass of something liquid and white.

"What is this?" I asked. "I'm not hungry. I'm going to bed."

"Drink it," Millie insisted. "A tough night can make for a fitful sleep. It'll help you rest."

I drank the warm frothy drink in four gulps. I thought it

was milk, but it tasted like something completely different. It was so good that I actually wished there were more.

"There isn't," Millie said. "Now go to sleep."

I walked slowly up the stairs and directly to my bedroom. I didn't bother to take off my shoes or wash up. I just dropped down onto my bed and let sleep do the rest.

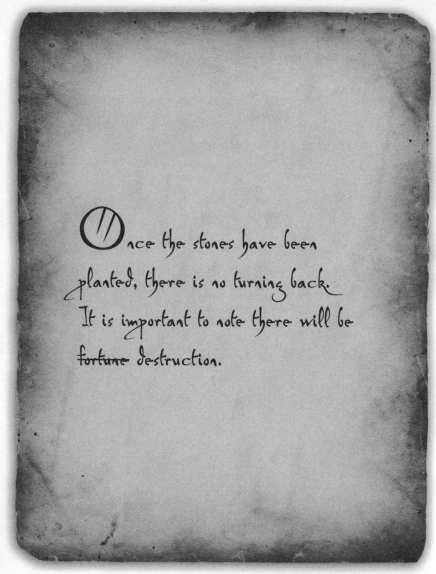

Once the stones have been planted, there is no turning back. It is important to note there will be ~~fortune~~ destruction.

CHAPTER 19

Tell Me Why

EVEN I WAS SURPRISED BY HOW long I slept. When I finally woke up, the sun was traveling back down and the clock said 3:17 P.M. The bright sunny day had almost completely passed me by.

"Wow," I said groggily. "What did Millie give me?"

I lay on my bed for half an hour more, just staring at the ceiling and trying to shake the cobwebs from my head. I thought about my dad and how ill he was. I thought about what I had done at the base of the elevator. And I thought about Kate and how much she was going to be hurt when she found out that I was lying to her.

"She has no right to be mad," I heard myself say. The words sounded selfish and mean and unlike anything I had ever said about Kate before. I sat up in bed and shook my head. "What's wrong with me?"

Mr. Binkers was sitting on my dresser staring at me.

"Don't judge me," I scolded him.

I wanted to throw something at him so he'd look away, but there was nothing to throw. I could feel my mind changing, and I didn't like it.

I got out of bed, took a shower, and then put on a white T-shirt with a picture of a squirrel on it. Thomas had bought the shirt for me in Kingsplot. He was not only the manager of the manor; he was also my personal shopper. Unfortunately for me and good fashion, he had horrible style. I couldn't tell if he thought I was really simple, or really dumb. I was the only kid at school who was happy we had a dress code. If I'd had to wear my casual clothes, I would have been beat up hundreds of times.

I slipped on my jeans and shoes and then headed to the narrow staircase. When I got to the fifth floor, it was just after four o'clock. I grabbed a flashlight from the tub, opened the closet door, and started to step in.

There was no elevator.

The elevator was gone, and all there was were long dark cables and an empty shaft. I had to grab onto the sides of the closet door to stop myself from falling in. I pushed back and stood there looking at where the elevator cart should be—someone had taken it down. I leaned over the edge of the floor and stared. There was no light, just the black cables stretching down into the darkness.

"This isn't good," I complained.

I looked around the inside of the shaft for any secondary button. There was nothing; there was no way to recall the elevator and command it to come back up.

"Dad," I whispered loudly. "He couldn't have."

I had no idea what to do. I ran downstairs to see if maybe Millie or Thomas or Wane had taken the elevator. Millie was in the kitchen with Wane.

"Feeling better?" Millie asked.

"Yeah," I said with worry. "Is Thomas around?"

"In his office," Wane said.

I checked to make sure Thomas was in his office and then climbed back up to the fifth floor. The elevator still wasn't there.

This wasn't good.

I started to worry about the people my father might have hurt to get out of the hospital and get here. I should have never told him about the elevator.

"Think, Beck, think," I ordered my brain.

I was scared of getting into trouble, but I was most

frightened about someone besides me being down there with the nesting dragon. I had planted it, and it belonged to me.

"Ahhhh!" I yelled.

My angst seemed to have some sort of control over the elevator because the moment I screamed, the cables began to move and groan as they pulled the elevator cart back up.

My heart jumped simultaneously with relief and fear. I needed the elevator back, but I wasn't necessarily prepared to confront whoever had taken it down. I closed the closet door so that whoever had used it wouldn't know I was on to them. I then looked for somewhere to hide. The windows had drapes, but they were thin and short. I shifted the chair that was in the lounging section of the bathroom and ducked behind it. With the closet door closed, I could just barely hear the cables working.

It seemed like forever, but eventually the sound of the elevator cart getting closer grew louder. I could hear it pull up and stop behind the door. It groaned, and then there was silence.

I gulped accordingly.

The doorknob rattled, and the door slowly squeaked open. From where I was, I couldn't see into the closet yet. I ducked down farther, hoping that whoever was there would just walk out without seeing me.

The door opened wider, and there were Kate and Wyatt.

I gasped so loudly that they both turned and looked directly at me. I don't think I would have been more shocked if it had been a dragon. I couldn't believe it.

"Beck?" Kate said with surprise.

Four things worried me: one, Kate and Wyatt had used the elevator without my permission; two, they were spending time together and leaving me out; three, Kate didn't look happy to see me; and four, I had not yet come up with a good story for why I had secretly been growing dragons down below. Instead of instantly begging for understanding, I decided to go with false indignation in an attempt to make them feel like the bad guys.

"What are you guys doing?" I said standing up straight. "This is my house."

"Too late, Beck," Kate said, disappointed. "We saw what was down there. How could you?"

False indignation wasn't working so I tried being contrite. "You don't understand, I had no choice," I pleaded. "My father made me do it."

Wyatt just stared at the ground as if for once in his life he realized that it wasn't his place to talk.

"Your father?" Kate said, sounding heartbroken. "Isn't he in Kingsplot?"

I nodded.

"How did he make you do it then, Beck?" Kate asked. "Did he force you to get the stone? Did he force you to plant it? Did he force you to gather all that water and all that food?"

Kate's blue eyes were wet at the edges. I couldn't stand it.

"Did he force you to lie to me?"

Wyatt started to quietly ease backward and out of the room.

"You don't understand," I argued.

"That's true," Kate said, standing up as tall as she could. "I don't understand how this could happen after all we've been through and everything that's happened to us. I don't understand why you would promise me one thing and do another. I don't understand how the boy I love could do this to me."

The word *love* made my heart start to rip itself apart in shame. I wanted to tell her how sorry I was, but the darkness easing into my brain was really bothered by her use of the word *boy*. The guilt and sorrow I felt in my heart were being buried by my brain. I should have listened to my heart, but my brain was gaining control.

"I'm sorry you don't understand, but you still don't have permission to be here," I said calmly. "I would have told you if you had given me time. You're the ones who are out of line."

"We came to get you," Kate explained, a frightening strength in her voice. "Millie said to come on up, but when we got to your room, you wouldn't wake up. We shook you pretty hard. So I figured I'd show Wyatt the elevator. When I saw the button glowing, we decided to press it. Sorry if you feel we crossed some sort of boundary. I know how strictly you follow rules."

"Not fair," I said selfishly. "You don't know what's happening."

"Really?" she said. "I think I have a pretty clear grip on what's happening. In fact, I can even see what's going to happen next."

"What?" I asked.

"I'm going to break up with you," she said seriously. "Good luck, Beck. I have a feeling you're going to need it."

"Kate," I lamely tried to debate. "Don't do this."

It was already done. Kate walked out the door and left me alone with a growing feeling that the entire world was against me.

"Whatever," I said, totally disgusted with myself and completely driven to carry on.

I stepped into the elevator and pushed the button.

I was going down.

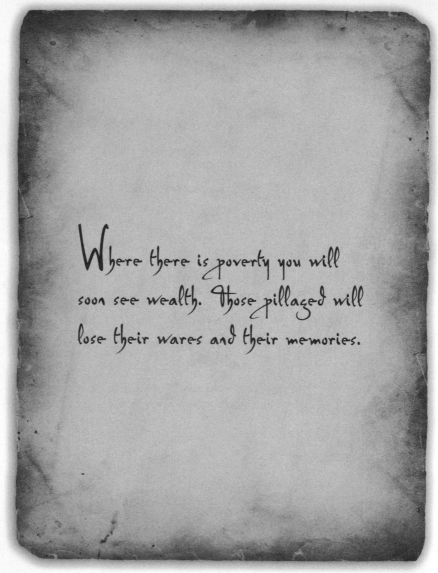

Where there is poverty you will soon see wealth. Those pillaged will lose their wares and their memories.

The beginning of section sixteen of The Grim Knot

CHAPTER 20

For No One

VERY FEW THINGS REALLY SURPRISE ME, but I was pretty surprised when two days later the stone hatched and, unlike the times before, I was right there when it happened. I was down in the glass cavern tending the closed and swollen nest and preparing more water and food. One moment I was stacking cans of food I had swiped from the kitchen when I looked over and the leafy pod began to open up. Three of the broad green leaves rippled and unfurled.

The cavern was suddenly filled with the sound of gurgling and popping. I couldn't decide if I should run toward the pod or away. The leaves shook and rolled open like the top of a tin sardine can. I could smell a sharp, pleasant odor like newly cut grass or fresh Christmas trees. The big pod bounced up and down and then, with a wet crack, it gushed open at the top and liquid of some sort flowed out. The pod then dropped and seemed to exhale. As it settled, a small dragon pushed out of the goo like a mountaineer cresting an impossibly tall mountain and tumbled from the nest onto the dirt. A dark mud formed around the small creature as it lay there taking long, deep gulps of air.

I stood there frozen from surprise.

The small dragon shifted in the dirt. I ran to the creature, not having any idea what to do. It was covered in slime and was already slightly imposing. It looked as though it was made of a mixture of stone and plastic. It was too big to pick up, so I knelt down next to it while talking softly.

"Hey, guy," I said, having no real idea if it was a girl or boy. "Don't worry; you're going to be fine."

The dragon was orange with a stark red streak running down its curved back. It looked like a wad of wriggling fire. Its face was long with a pointed snout and deep-set green eyes. I had raised a number of dragons, but I had never seen one so new. I was about to get some water and offer it to the small creature, but I was stopped by the noise of the nest gurgling again. I looked over and saw the leafy pod shake and twitch. Another leafy fold drew back and the head of a second dragon popped out of the sticky mess and tumbled to the dirt.

The surprise was almost debilitating.

I staggered and tried to steady myself. I was confident that I had planted only one stone, and yet here was a second dragon. All of the rocks I had previously sown had produced single dragons, but I was seeing double. The second one was yellow, and had a broad maroon streak running down its back. It too was covered in goo.

"Towels," I said, trying to regain my composure. "I need some towels."

As I stood, I watched the first dragon push up on its front legs and shift closer to its companion. He started to lick the yellow one, cleaning the goo from its back.

"Ewww," I said, disgusted. "That's repulsive."

Despite the disgust, the two little dragons gave me a great sense of happiness. Joy rushed up over me. I felt like I had done something important, something that would make all those like Kate and my father reevaluate how they were treating me.

"Names," I said, looking at the two dragons. "You two need names. How about . . ."

Before I could even begin to label them the nest moaned and popped once more.

"Uh-oh," I whispered.

Four huge leafy folds split open and the center of the nest boiled up into a bubble. The bubble grew until it was three feet high and then with one frightening pop it burst, sending goo all over the glass cavern. I wiped my eyes clear and there before me was a third dragon falling out of the pod.

This dragon was different than the other two. Not only was it jet black, but it was much bigger. It had a ring of small uneven bumps around its large forehead and right ear, making it look like it was wearing a jaunty crown. Its legs were muscular and long and its arms were streaked with thick black hair.

The two smaller dragons immediately shifted toward the new arrival and began licking and cleaning. The black beast was so mesmerizing that I was almost drawn into licking it off as well. It had wide orange eyes and a long neck. Small spikes ran down its lower back and onto its split tail. I didn't really want to play favorites, but I knew immediately that I liked the black one best.

The large dragon pushed its front end up with its arms and steadied its wobbling head. I was tempted to reach out and touch it, but the temptation vanished when it opened its mouth and let out a terrifying screech. I covered my ears, thinking the glass cavern would shatter. The dragon then closed its mouth and looked at me as if expecting something.

"Yes?" I asked.

It continued to stare at me while the two smaller ones worked to clean it off.

"Water?" I guessed.

I ran and got a bucket of water and set it down. I don't want

to embarrass myself, but I think I might have curtsied right after giving it to him.

The black dragon screamed and then took a long, lusty
drink. It pushed up on its back legs and wobbled on all fours.
The two other ones did the same thing, keeping close to his
sides and continuing to clean him.

I leaned to my left and took a closer look at the leafy pod
they had just emerged from. It was now completely deflated and
lying on the ground like a mound of soggy seaweed.

"Three dragons," I said in awe. "That's a surprise."

The Grim Knot had never said a thing about the last dragon
being more than one. Of course, the authors of *The Grim Knot*
had never really experienced the last dragon. That part was for
me to finish someday. And, whereas I typically needed to write
things down so I wouldn't forget them, I had a feeling that I
would never forget the fact that these three dragons had come
from one stone.

I stared at them all, feeling a strange strength and power
rising in my chest. There was no part of me that wanted to
share this with anyone—not with my father, not Kate and Wyatt,
no one. The moment felt intimate and intoxicating and personal.

The black dragon stumbled two steps closer to me and lowered its head slightly. I reached out and touched him on the
left ear. His skin felt warm and rough and wet. The orange and

yellow dragons saw what was happening, and the backs of their necks rankled.

"I'm not hurting him," I told them. "See."

I touched the black dragon on the forehead and then on the back of his long neck. The orange one hissed and then backed away.

I laughed out loud.

I had to believe that the rest of the world would have loved to be where I was and see what I saw. Dragons were a myth, a story, and a lie. But I knew different. I knew they were as real as any other creature. And I knew that my family was the key and the connection to keeping them alive. There was no way I could destroy these. I would raise them and then hide them wherever necessary to protect them. Their survival depended on me, and I wouldn't let them down.

I petted the heads of all three dragons one by one.

"Don't worry," I consoled them. "I'm not going to let anything happen to you."

The dragons moved their legs and arms, stretching and screaming. All three had wings, but none of them could open them fully yet. The orange and yellow ones had black claws and beet-red mouths. When they opened their jaws to scream or squawk, their tongues looked like red chilies. The black one's tongue was blue and long and curled at the end when he rolled it out.

In the past it had been kind of difficult to name the dragons. Not because I couldn't come up with ideas, but because I always had to make sure Kate and Wyatt agreed. Now, the task belonged to just me and I already knew just what I wanted to call them.

The one with the red stripe reminded me of a redheaded kid I once knew named Paul. He was a tough kid who was always hitting people and things. So I felt his name might work perfectly— Paul. The yellow one was Malcolm because it sounded tough, and the large black one was Jude because I had wanted to name one of the previous dragons Jude, and Kate had said no.

The trio of dragons moved carefully closer to the soggy pod. Jude opened his jaws and began to devour the very nest of leaves he had come from. After he had taken a few large bites, Jude raised his head and signaled Paul and Malcolm to join him. All three chewed and tore at the nest until there was nothing left.

I had never seen any dragons do that.

"I have a feeling you're going to show me a lot of things I've never seen before," I said to them.

Jude screeched, and Paul and Malcolm followed suit as my mind continued to grow just a bit darker.

"I can't believe Kate doesn't want this," I said to Jude.

He ignored me and bent down to drink another full bucket of water.

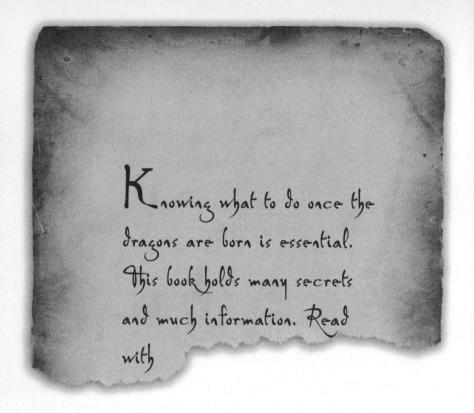

Knowing what to do once the dragons are born is essential. This book holds many secrets and much information. Read with

The beginning of section seventeen of The Grim Knot

CHAPTER 21

The Long, Winding Road

EVEN SUSPENSION WAS WORKING OUT great for me. In fact, the last week of my being suspended was one of my favorite weeks ever. Okay, I did feel sick about Kate and me splitting up, but I had things to take my mind off of it—things like dragons.

Jude, Paul, and Malcolm were more entertaining than the other dragons I had raised. Paul and Malcolm followed Jude everywhere, acting like his own personal bodyguards. They let him eat first, dug spots in the dirt for him to sleep, and kept an eye on me constantly. I had the feeling that if Jude didn't trust me, I would be in big trouble. But, Jude did trust me; he stayed by me like an old family dog. Whenever I was down in the glass cavern, he was attentive and obedient to everything I said.

It wasn't all fun. They were going through food and water

quickly. I had planned on taking care of only one dragon. I was collecting and bringing whatever I could find for them to eat, but I knew I could only keep it up a few more days before they were out of food and looking at me as more of a snack than a zookeeper. Plus, Millie was getting suspicious of the snacks and food that were disappearing from the pantry. I kept telling her that she was just getting old and had lost track, but she wasn't buying it.

My biggest concern was the size of the dragons. They were bulking up quickly. The glass cavern could still fit them, but there was only one way out, the elevator. I knew that once they were too big to be transported in the elevator, they would be trapped down there forever. I was pretty sure I couldn't keep feeding and hiding them down there for much longer. I figured I had about a week before they were too big to transport up. So, consequently, I had about a week to find a new spot to keep them.

One of the nicest things about me taking care of the dragons was that I had been so busy I hadn't had time to bother Millie and Wane, or cause any trouble for Thomas around the manor. All three of them thought I was just spending time in my room and working on the huge pile of homework my teachers had sent with Kate.

I missed Kate, but I stubbornly knew she was wrong and I

was right. She knew how important this was. She knew that my family had an obligation. And she had to know that there really was no way for me to simply sit back and ignore the drive inside me. Yep, she was being stubborn.

Wyatt had called me the day after Kate and he left the manor. He said he wanted to help me clear things up, but I know he just wanted to stop me—to control me and make me feel bad about what I was destined to do. The phone conversation didn't go well. In fact, it ended with the two of us yelling at each other.

Big deal.

I couldn't control how selfish other people were. They could be helping me and experiencing what I was. Instead, they were all choosing the weak way out.

Because I had been so good, Thomas and Millie agreed to let me take the school bus to and from school once I was reinstated in school. I was still grounded, but they were going to allow me that. It was nice of them, but I knew that deep down they were just trying to get out of having to drive me.

So, the Monday after my three-week suspension I was standing out at the front gate of the manor, hoping that the dragons would do all right without me for the day. I had left them as much water and hay as I could possibly get them. I was also hoping that school wouldn't be too painful. I hadn't really been back since the bus incident, and then there had been that corn-stalk problem. I usually felt good knowing that at least I would have Kate and Wyatt on my side, but now I didn't have that.

"Whatever," I said, trying to act tough.

The bus pulled up to the gate, and the door opened. I hadn't been on a school bus since I had almost died on one. I was surprised to feel a little leery. I climbed up the few steps, and the door closed behind me.

"Morning, Beck," the bus driver, Steven, said nervously.

I didn't take it personally, seeing as Steven was nervous about everything. He was the last person I thought should ever drive a bus with kids on it.

There were only a few people on the bus so far. I could see Kate sitting near the back next to a girl named Mindy. As I was walking down the aisle I heard a big kid with bad teeth say, "I wonder what he'll screw up today?"

I walked past without talking back to him. I was a bit off my game. Normally I would have never let a comment like that go without saying something, but I needed to keep my nose clean.

I walked past Kate, keeping my eyes up and facing forward. I could see she was consciously gazing out the window so she didn't have to look at me. It bothered me that she looked so pretty.

I sat down in the back row and threw my backpack into the seat next to me to make sure nobody would sit there—it really wasn't necessary, seeing as nobody would want to anyway.

The bus stopped and picked up a few more kids. A couple of stops later, we had our full load and began heading down the winding mountain road into Kingsplot. I looked at everyone on the bus and tried to figure out where I fit in. I didn't want to go back to school, and I had thought it would be nice not to be driven and lectured by Thomas, but now the bus felt so uncomfortable and hostile. I knew I had made mistakes, but I was beginning to feel like people were treating me unfairly. I hated the feeling in my mind.

It was about a thirty-minute drive down the steep, twisty road before we reached the edge of Kingsplot. Students were talking and laughing as Steven carefully drove. Kate was two benches up, talking to Mindy. I couldn't clearly hear what they were saying, but I heard the word *prom*.

My chest tightened with embarrassment. I felt like a jerk for hurting Kate, but part of me was happy that we weren't going. It was she that had broken up with me, and now she wouldn't get to go to prom because of it.

Kate said something about buying a dress.

I leaned forward and tried to listen closely. I figured Kate had just bought a dress for something normal. I mean, I'm not a girl, but I know that sometimes they buy dresses.

" . . . Wyatt's taking . . ."

Wyatt was taking someone to the prom? That was more than a little surprising to me. I knew Wyatt wanted to go, but I couldn't imagine who he had tricked into going with him.

"He's picking me up . . ."

Some skinny kids with matching blond hair were talking too loudly for me to eavesdrop properly. I was getting bits and pieces, but none of it made sense. My mind was busily trying to piece together all the words I had heard—*dress, Wyatt, picking*. The only way I could string the words was in a way that didn't make any sense and made me sick. Kate was going to the prom with Wyatt?

The thought was absurd. It was like hearing someone say that all dogs now loved cats. I couldn't believe it. I listened more.

"It'll be fun," Kate said. ". . . good memory . . ."

Good memory? That was the line I had used on her. I was the one who had informed her of the fact.

I don't know what got into me, but suddenly my hands were opening and closing, and the back of my neck felt like it was two hundred degrees. My eyes grew blurry, and when I blinked, all I could see was red. I felt like I was turning into a much skinnier, paler version of The Hulk.

I stood and stomped up two rows. I looked down at Kate.

She didn't look surprised at all to see me, which made me even madder.

"You're going to the prom with Wyatt?" I asked, hating the way I sounded and hoping she would respond by laughing at how absurd the idea was.

"I don't know why that's any of your business," Kate said coolly, her blue eyes looking directly into my brown.

I looked away from her gaze.

"This was your choice," Kate said without emotion.

"You broke up with me," I argued. "I think that was your choice."

"Don't be dumb, Beck," she said, trying to keep her voice down as everyone around us stared. "You know what happened."

"Beck, have a seat," Steven yelled as timidly as he could from the driver's seat. "All students are to stay seated."

I kept standing.

"Take your seat," he yelled a bit louder.

I looked up the aisle toward the driver. Steven had his

hands on the big steering wheel, and his eyes were facing forward. He looked up at the rearview mirror, and I could see his
eyes.

"Take your seat," he insisted.

I sat down in the empty seat across from Kate.

"Can't we talk about this?" I asked, my brain clearing just
enough to know that I didn't want it to end this way. I loved
Kate, and she was very important to me. I knew that, but I was
just having a horrible time convincing my mind to act right.

Kate turned in her seat so that her legs were in the aisle and
she was facing me. She leaned her head in closer as I did the
same. Our noses were now only a couple of inches away.

"Listen," she whispered fiercely. "I don't know what you're
doing, but you had better think long and hard about it. It's not
just you that could be in danger."

"There's no danger," I whispered back. "It's different this
time."

"It's not," Kate said sadly. "You're wrong, Beck, I . . ."

I'd like to think that she was just about to say, "You're
wrong, Beck, I love you," but I'll never know because at that
exact moment the bus swerved slightly, making all of us fall
against each other.

"Sorry," Steven yelled back.

I looked out the back window, and there, lying on the road,

was a single tree. Steven had barely missed it. I turned back to Kate as everyone laughed about Steven's driving.

"Can we at least talk about all this?" I asked.

Kate opened her mouth, but before anything came out, the bus swerved again, this time sending us all sliding to the right and up against each other. Everyone started yelling Steven's name and complaining.

I looked out the back window again. Standing in the middle of the road was a single pine tree. Unlike the first tree, however, this one was upright.

Every hair on the back of my neck and arms stood up and screamed. Something was wrong. I looked over at Kate and tried to warn her.

"I think we're in trouble."

At that moment the bus hit what felt like two big speed bumps in a row. We all bounced up and down. One of the really skinny kids in the second row flew all the way to the roof and banged his head.

I looked out the back window and saw two thin trees lying straight across the road like barriers. Kids were screaming and yelling things about Steven's driving performance and what their parents were going to do when they told them.

"Everyone calm down!" Steven yelled. "There's some debris in the road."

Kate looked at me as if this were my fault. "What's happening?" she asked.

"I have no idea," I said sort of truthfully.

Two large objects hit the top of the bus, creating two huge dents. The noise of the impact popped everyone's ears and signaled to most of us to stop holding back and scream with all our might.

The two trees flew off the roof and rolled behind us. The long bus screeched around a tight turn, and as I was looking out the window, I witnessed a thick pine tree hurling toward the vehicle.

"Look out!" I yelled.

The tree slammed into the bus, cracking two windows and lifting the vehicle a couple of inches on the right side. The tires came down, and the whole bus skidded in the other direction. I could see Steven desperately trying to keep control of the steering wheel.

"Stop the bus!" I screamed, wondering why Steven hadn't already done so.

Apparently the students in the bus finally agreed with me about something because everyone began to scream the same thing.

"Stop the bus!"

I could see how violently Steven was wrestling with the

steering wheel, and I couldn't understand why he wasn't stopping. My heart went out to him, having already been through my own bus ordeal. I didn't feel just panic, I felt empathy. Another tree hit the opposite side of the bus. The crown of the tree shot through one of the windows and poked inside. It narrowly missed a couple of students.

There was a new kind of screaming now as everyone moved away from the windows and into the aisle, all the while yelling, "Stop the bus!"

A few of the tougher kids were adding swear words to their request, and some were hollering, "Landslide!"

I knew that to those on the bus it seemed like the only explanation, but I also knew the truth. This wasn't a landslide. Once again, nature was out to get me. Because the stone had already been planted and the dragons had hatched, I knew that wasn't the cause. That meant the trees were out to take care of me—to kill me. I couldn't easily see what my death would do for them, but then it struck me.

"They want the dragons," I said aloud.

"What?" Kate asked, as she was balled up behind the seat.

The road straightened out, and I could see through the front window that we were about to enter one of the few stone tunnels that the road traveled through. I thought that if we could reach the tunnel and stop inside we might be safe from falling trees for a while.

I frantically climbed over the seats and backs of students to make my way to the front. Steven was still wrestling with the steering wheel.

"Stop in the tunnel!" I yelled at him.

"I can't!" he yelled back.

"You have to," I said. "We'll be safe."

"No," Steven hollered. "I can't, the brakes aren't working. Something happened when we hit those trees."

The students nearest the front heard what Steven said and passed the news along in screams and yelps.

"Push the brakes harder!" I told him, knowing personally how hard it was to stop a moving bus.

Two of the back windows burst apart as small stones broke through the window. The trees were throwing rocks. We had to stop the bus in the tunnel or we would be beaten apart.

"Stop the bus!" everyone yelled.

I watched a dozen trees on the cliff in front of us rip themselves from the walls and dive down to the road we were about to drive over. The trees fell on the ground in straight lines, and the bus drove right over them, bumping and bouncing like a wild horse.

The tunnel was only a few hundred feet away now.

"Stop the bus, Steven!" I pleaded.

"I can't stop it!" Steven cried. "It won't stop!"

We shot into the tunnel, and everything grew dim. Everyone shut up, and for a few moments it was almost quiet as the bus hurled forward.

I could hear myself breathing heavily, and sweat was running down my forehead into my eyes. I thought about just opening the door and jumping out. If it was me that the trees were after, then the rest of the bus might be okay. Of course, if that happened then I might die and my dragons would be left to perish underground.

I couldn't let that happen.

We shot out of the tunnel and continued to hurl rapidly down the mountain road. We were going fast, but Steven was doing a pretty good job keeping us on the road. This section had very few trees growing on the cliffs and for the moment nothing was hitting the bus or coming down on us. Students began to shift and move back to their seats as they whimpered and moaned.

"Are we okay?" the big kid who had been such a jerk to me earlier asked me as I stood next to Steven.

"I think so," I replied.

Steven was sweating like a cold glass of water on a hot day. His entire face was dripping perspiration.

I glanced down the winding road and could see the second tunnel. I knew that a couple of miles below that tunnel there was a giant rocky section that would slow the bus down perfectly if we drove into it.

"Hold on!" I told Steven. "After that tunnel is that rocky section. That'll stop us."

Steven actually looked relieved as he pulled the steering wheel hard to the right to keep us in our lane.

"Just keep the bus on the road until we get to those rocks."

I held onto the railing behind the driver's seat and kept my eyes locked forward. Not a single tree or rock had assaulted us since we had come out of the first tunnel. I was hoping that maybe those trees were just warning me and that there would be no more problems today.

Steven pulled the wheel to the left and everyone onboard flew to the side. They weren't screaming any longer. It seemed as if we all knew how important it was for Steven to concentrate.

The bus was gaining speed and each turn felt more violent than the last, but I could see the tunnel and knew we had a chance. Steven yanked the wheel to the right one more time and then straightened the vehicle out.

The tunnel was up ahead.

All of us held our breath as the bus sped into the tunnel.

It was dim again, and I turned around and hollered out some instructions.

"We just have to make it to the rocky field!" I yelled. "Everyone duck down behind their seats when we get there."

I really had no idea if that was what we should do, but when Kate and I had been traveling on that falling train, we had ducked down, and we were still alive. So I figured it wouldn't hurt us to try that again.

The bus shot out of the tunnel. We were getting lower on the mountain now, and there were clouds just fifty feet above us. I couldn't see very far ahead, but I knew that the rocky section of land was only a few miles farther.

Steven spun the wheel and pulled us safely through another sharp turn.

"We're going to make it," he said, exhaling.

Everyone on board began chanting Steven's name.

"Steven, Steven, Steven!"

I turned and smiled at the group, and then swiveled to look ahead. We were not going to make it. Hundreds of pine trees were dropping out of the clouds and raining down on the road in front of us. It looked like the whole forest had ripped free from the ground and was now descending on us. We were nowhere near safety, and we were being ambushed.

I screamed so that others would know they should too.

Steven kept his hands on the wheel and closed his eyes. Trees bombarded the bus, slamming through windows and pounding the top like a group of angry gorillas. The bus flew up and down as it bounced over trees in the road. Rocks pelted the sides and top of the bus, cracking and splitting all of the windows. Steven ducked as a massive tree trunk flew sideways into the front window, blowing the glass back and over all of us. I opened my eyes and could see the rocky field just off to the side.

"Pull in!" I screamed.

Steven turned the wheel slightly, and the bus jumped off the road and careened into the rocky field. The rocky ground grabbed the bus tires and slowed it down within a few hundred feet. Everyone flew toward me and then snapped back. I lost my grip on the rail and ended up in a ball on the steps in front of the door.

Most students got as close to the floor as they could, with their arms and backpacks over their heads. Trees and rocks continued to fall from above. I looked up at Steven. He still had his hands on the wheel and was staring forward, mumbling something incoherent.

I was wondering how much longer it would be until the roof of the bus was broken and we all died, when the large hits and thumps finally began to slow.

"It's stopping!" someone yelled.

I didn't know if that was true, so I kept cowering on the bus steps. I couldn't hear anything but the sound of students crying and whimpering. I figured there were no more trees above us that could fall or push stones.

Steven reached down, and I took his hand. I stood up and looked back at the rest of the bus. I saw Kate close to where she had been at the beginning. Her eyes locked with mine. She not only looked upset, but she looked out for blood—my blood.

The roof of the bus was beat down so low I could barely stand up. There wasn't a single window still intact, and three trees had worked themselves completely into the space. The bus was blanketed with trees that were hanging off the roof and covering many of the windows. Nobody was seriously hurt, but I could tell most of the kids would be emotionally scarred for years.

We all waited in the bus for help. It came pretty quickly as cars coming up the highway had been stopped by trees on the road and the people had spotted the bus in the rocky field.

We were all looked over and checked by EMTs. Those kids who were scraped or bruised got bandages and ointments, while people like me just got ignored.

I tried to get to Kate to talk to her, but she was being cared for by some tall, good-looking paramedic wearing a bandana.

Nobody besides me and Kate had any real explanation for what had happened. A landslide seemed like the most logical explanation—not real logical, but the most. The landscape was littered with pine trees. They were all over the road and had covered the bus like a woody Snuggie.

It took a while to clear enough trees off the pavement so that cars could move up and down the road, but eventually students began to be transported to their houses or places of safety. I was wondering how I would get back to the manor when a strong hand from behind patted me on the shoulder.

I turned around to find Sheriff Pax.

"Beck," he said sternly.

"Sheriff," I replied.

Sheriff Pax looked around at all the trees and destruction. "What a scene," he said. "So peculiar."

"Yeah," I said lamely.

"Guess who gets to drive you home?" he asked.

I moaned.

"What's the matter?" Sheriff Pax asked. "It'll give us some time to talk about this."

I moaned again.

"Oh, and we'll be taking the Figgins's girl as well," he added. "I have a few questions for her also."

I moaned for the third time as Sheriff Pax led me to his car. Kate was already in the backseat waiting. She didn't even look up as I slid in next to her.

Something in my life needed to change.

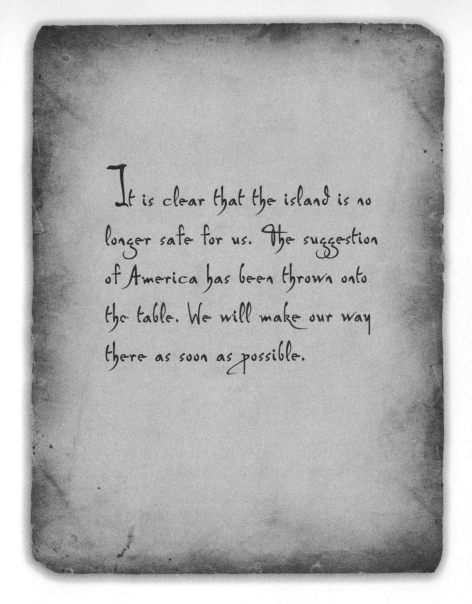

It is clear that the island is no longer safe for us. The suggestion of America has been thrown onto the table. We will make our way there as soon as possible.

The beginning of section eighteen of The Grim Knot

CHAPTER 22

The Fool on the Hill

RIDING IN CARS WITH ADULTS can be painful and uncomfortable. I should know because I have been on a lot of uncomfortable car rides before. The one with Sheriff Pax and Kate, however, ranks among the top most uncomfortable moments of my whole life. Kate wasn't talking, but I could tell she was very close to just blurting out everything about me—dragons and all—and how horrible I was. I give credit to her, however; she didn't say a word about it no matter how much Sheriff Pax questioned her. Since Kate wasn't going to spill anything, he went after me, hoping that I might say something that would motivate Kate to speak up.

Adding to the overall feeling of worry was the fact that we were now driving back up the same road we had just been attacked on. I kept looking out the window, praying the forest was done with the ambush.

"Now, you two are close," the sheriff said, sounding like an adult being forced to speak about an awkward subject.

"Not anymore," I said. "Kate's going to the prom with Wyatt."

I could see the sheriff's face in the rearview mirror. He looked like a man that wanted to talk about almost anything else.

"Well, you *were* close," he clarified.

"*Were,*" Kate emphasized.

"What do you think just happened?" the sheriff asked. "Did those trees just fall from the sky?"

I stayed silent so that Kate could answer. Even in moments of trial I was quite the gentleman.

"Beck?" Sheriff Pax asked.

"No," I said. "Trees don't just fall from the sky. It was a landslide."

"Landslides involve sliding mud and soil."

"Not all landslides are created equal," I pointed out.

"This was not a landslide," Sheriff Pax said, bothered by my insolence. "People could have died. Another bus was ruined."

"That wasn't my fault," I argued.

"I'm not so sure," he said.

"Kate, what do you think of all this?"

"I think we're lucky to be alive," she said solemnly.

"She's always really positive," I added.

"I'm trying to do my job, Beck," Sheriff Pax begged. "I can't decide if I should arrest you."

"For what?" I said. "For helping Steven stop that bus?"

"Kate," he pleaded. "Do you remember the time the dragons attacked?"

"Yes," Kate said. "Everyone does."

"That's not true," Sheriff Pax insisted. "I barely remember it and, according to Beck, I helped you all escape. Nobody seems to remember any solid details. Not only are there no details in Kingsplot, but it seems as though those outsiders who reported on it now believe it never happened. There were videos that are gone, pictures that have faded, and nobody seems to care."

"You do," Kate said quietly.

"I do," Sheriff Pax said passionately. "But I have to write things down just to be able to remember them the next day. It's taken me months of daily reminders to convince myself that if something happens that involves plants, Beck might be to blame."

"Well, that's rude," I said.

"I want to help this town," Sheriff Pax said. "Help me help you."

I laughed, thinking his last words sounded really cheesy.

"Why do the plants attack?" he asked.

"I don't know, they just do," I said. "I can't explain it."

"Are there more dragons?"

"Dragons aren't real," I told him.

"Is something about to happen?"

"Yes," I replied. "You're about to drop us off at our houses."

"Did you know that not many months ago a woman on the other side of the mountains was practicing the organ in a church when the roof was ripped off and the entire place was set on fire?"

I kept silent, knowing all too well about the incident he was referring to and wondering if he had forgotten he was involved.

"I was the one covering that case," he continued. "I have a file on it that shows pictures of the burnt church, and there's a statement from the woman that says she saw a dragon rip the roof off."

"Wow," I replied. I was really commenting on how well his mind had done at forgetting.

"I don't remember that at all," he said. "In fact, while reading the file, I thought it was a joke or a prank. But then on the bottom of the file on a Post-it note was the word *Beck*."

"There's a musician by that name," I told him. "Maybe you were referring to him."

"I don't think so."

We reached the gate to the Pillage manor, and Sheriff Pax passed it up.

"I think I'll drop Miss Figgins off first if you don't mind, Beck."

"Not at all," I said.

When we reached Kate's house, she got out, thanked the sheriff for the ride, and then walked briskly to her house. We watched her open the front door and disappear inside.

Sheriff Pax turned the car around and drove back toward the manor.

"Beck, I need your help," he said.

"You've mentioned that," I replied. "But I'm not sure what you want. I'm just a kid. You're the sheriff."

"Is something bad about to happen?"

"Yes," I said again. "Millie and Thomas are going to be mad that I'm home again."

"Always a joke," the sheriff complained.

"I see you remember that," I pointed out.

"Your father isn't doing well," he said seriously, changing the subject.

"How do you know?"

"I went to visit him yesterday," he said. "They have him in solitary confinement. He seemed out of sorts and hostile."

"He probably just hates policemen," I said. "A lot of people do. You should probably leave him alone."

"I don't plan to leave anyone alone until I figure out what is happening here," the sheriff said. "Do you understand?"

"I know I'm just a kid," I said, "but I understand. You need to understand this, though; my father isn't well, and you've no right to bother him."

"He said you had betrayed him," Sheriff Pax said. He threw that bit of information out as if it were a secret he had been holding for the right moment.

"He did not," I argued.

"He did," the sheriff said. "He said he had you come to get him out and then you turned on him and told them he was crazy."

"I never did that!"

"He said you stole something from him."

I kept quiet, wondering just how much my father had told him.

"But when I pressed him, he said you took his rock," the sheriff said, disjointed. "He's not in the best frame of mind."

"Well, there you have it," I said. "My father's not well."

Sheriff Pax pulled past the gate and drove up the drive.

"It really is quite a place you live in," the sheriff said in awe. "I bet there's no other manor in the world as amazing as this."

"That's probably true," I said, feeling proud.

"Funny, I've never seen it mentioned in any articles or seen any pictures of it on the Internet."

"Why would there be?" I asked, wanting him to just hurry and pull up to the manor so I could get out.

"The world loves architecture," the sheriff explained. "It just seems as though there would be a number of people interested in this place."

"We're kinda off the beaten path," I pointed out.

"That's true," Sheriff Pax said. "But combined with the rumors of dragons, this should be like Area 51."

"People used to come around," I said defensively, feeling as if he were ripping on the manor. "They used to try and get to the back gardens and look at the conservatory."

"Why?" Sheriff Pax asked.

"You really need to take some sort of pill that helps you with your memory," I said. "That's where the dragons were raised, of course."

Sheriff Pax stopped the car in the courtyard and put it in park. He didn't get out to open my door for me. Instead he picked up a notebook from the passenger seat and scribbled something in it.

"I need to tell you something," he said seriously. "I'm going to request that you not attend school the rest of the year."

"What?" I asked, both angry and relieved.

"I can't be sure that you didn't have something to do with what happened today," he explained. "A lot of people could have been seriously hurt."

"So I won't graduate?" I asked with concern.

"I'll get Principal Wales to gather all your work," he said, as if that would comfort me. "You'll graduate, but you won't be attending."

"What happens if tomorrow the bus is attacked when I'm not on it?"

"I'd be surprised," he said. "You and I both know that what happened today had everything to do with you. Now the challenge for me is to make sure I don't forget it."

"When people get older, like you, it gets hard to remember." I wasn't trying to be mean, it was just some useless thought I didn't have the willpower to keep to myself.

"Thanks," Sheriff Pax said sternly.

"You're welcome."

Sheriff Pax closed his notebook and set it back down in the passenger seat. He stared out the front window at the manor for a few seconds before speaking.

"Do you mind if I look around?" he asked. "It's been a while since I've wandered your grounds."

"I guess not," I replied, shrugging. "Knock yourself out."

Sheriff Pax looked at me strangely, and then got out of the car and opened my door. I stepped out and thanked him.

"I'd tip you," I said, "but Thomas stopped my allowance because of what happened at the museum."

Sheriff Pax put his right hand on my left shoulder.

"Beck, I'm going to figure this out," he said honestly. "Kingsplot means too much to me to let it go."

"Good luck," I said nicely. "I'm rooting for you to come to your senses."

"You could make it easier," he told me.

"Yeah," I replied kindly. "But that's not really my style."

Sheriff Pax smiled.

"Something about you impresses me," he said. "But something bigger concerns me."

"You're a complicated man," I pointed out.

Sheriff Pax walked over toward the garage as I walked into the back service door to try and explain to Millie why I was home early.

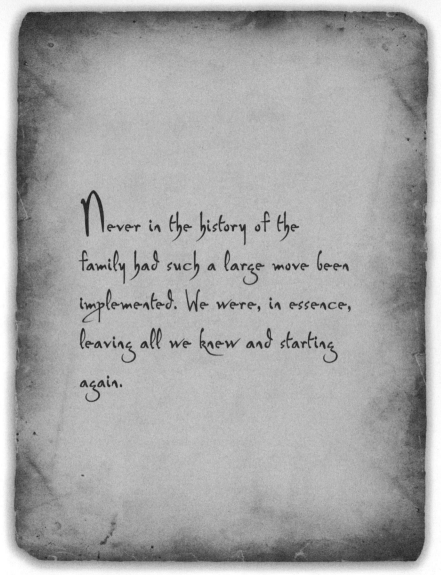

Never in the history of the family had such a large move been implemented. We were, in essence, leaving all we knew and starting again.

The beginning of section nineteen of The Grim Knot

CHAPTER 23

You Can't Do That

BELIEVE IT OR NOT, I WAS VERY happy to be forcedly home-schooled. There were only a few weeks left of school, and I was more than willing to do all my learning right in the manor. I spent an hour the next morning doing homework in the kitchen with Millie and Wane. I needed their help with geometry, but they had more questions about what had happened yesterday than math assistance.

"The trees just fell from the sky?" Wane asked.

"No," I replied, wondering why everyone liked to ask that. "They fell from the cliffs."

"Don't be smart," Millie said.

"What should I be, then?"

"Beck, we're concerned," Millie said, ignoring me. "Your father's not available to even talk to. I know that if he were, he'd have instructions regarding what to do with you because of what happened."

"Can't we just act like we did when I first moved here?" I begged. "Remember how we never talked about anything?"

"We want you to be safe," Wane said compassionately.

"I don't know what happened yesterday, but I know that I seem to have no problems while I'm here in the manor," I pointed out. "And since I'm probably never going to get to go anywhere else, I should be fine."

"You'll be extra careful and watchful?" Millie asked.

"Of course," I promised.

"That's a good boy," Millie said, handing me a plateful of cookies.

Wane put her curiosity aside and helped me with my homework for another hour. I then told them I had reading homework to do and headed back up to the fifth floor. I grabbed a flashlight, opened the closet, hopped into the elevator, and pushed the button.

All three dragons were waiting for me as I got off the elevator. Jude was strong and so cool-looking. His jet black skin and orange eyes made me wish I could show him off somewhere or enter him into a contest. Paul and Malcolm were cool but in a different way. They were so similar looking. The only real difference was their coloring. They were also more mischievous and unbridled. They screamed and tussled with each other constantly. Jude would always just look as if he were above all that.

Jude was roughly the size of a small horse now. In the last couple of days he had begun to open and exercise his wings. They too were jet black with orange at the tips, and when he flapped them, it felt like he could grasp the dirt and lift the entire earth out of orbit. I knew that now was the time to move them; by tomorrow it might be too late.

I still had no great idea where to put them. I halfway wished I had planted them in the train cave, but it was so far away and it would have taken too much effort to get to. And hauling food up there would have been almost impossible. I thought about moving them up to the seventh floor of the manor. If I put them in the big hall of the east wing they might go unnoticed for an afternoon. I had no real solution, so I figured I would just take them deep into the forest and make sure they were tied up so they couldn't travel too far. If I got them beyond the boulder field, there was a small grove that would hide them from everyone. It wasn't a perfect solution, but it was the best I could think of.

Millie and Thomas were going into Kingsplot in the afternoon to take care of some legal matters for my father. Wane would be gone as well with her boyfriend. So now felt like the perfect time to move the dragons. Scott was a problem, but he was supposedly working on repairing part of the stable roof. If I took the dragons out the east end, he would never see anything.

I returned to my room and waited for Millie and Thomas to leave. I stood by my window and witnessed Wane getting picked up and driving off.

It was now or never.

I went down to the glass cavern and tried to explain to the dragons what was happening.

"We're going someplace better," I said. "But I'll have to take you one at a time."

They seemed fine with it, but I could tell they also didn't really understand.

I knew that Paul and Malcolm would freak out if I took Jude first, so the plan was to take Malcolm, then Jude, and finally Paul.

"This is going to be great," I said putting my left arm around Malcolm's neck and leading him toward the elevator.

He followed me into the elevator without making any fuss. The fit inside the elevator was tight but we both squeezed in. I turned on the flashlight hanging from the ceiling and adjusted the light. Everything was running smoothly until I pressed the button. The metal gate dropped, and the elevator wheezed and began to lift. Malcolm pushed at the walls and dug his right wing into my stomach.

"Easy, Malcolm," I said. "This will just take a few minutes."

Malcolm snorted repeatedly as if he were on the verge of hyperventilating. He rocked on his feet and blinked his blue eyes rapidly. He opened his jaw, and his long red tongue rolled out and hung from the side of his mouth as he panted.

"It's going to be fine," I comforted, patting him on his scaly yellow neck.

The truth is, I could tell it wasn't going to be fine. Each inch we ascended, Malcolm became more and more agitated. He snapped at me twice, and by the time we had lifted high enough to be above ground, he was screeching and pulling at the metal gate. He kept trying to open his wings and jump through the ceiling. The flashlight was knocked about, giving the elevator a sort of strobe-light feel. He tore my shirt in half, ripped the right knee of my jeans, and dug a long scratch on my left arm. I started screaming louder than he was, begging him to knock it off. I was scared that his struggling and fighting would break the small elevator apart or strand us mid-floors.

"Please, Malcolm," I pleaded. "Hang on."

Just as the elevator was about to come apart at the corners, we lifted above the fourth floor and came to a stop at the fifth. I threw open the gate and pushed the closet door open. Malcolm didn't waste a second; he burst from the elevator and into the bathroom. He thrashed around, slipping on the tile floor and trying to figure out just where he was.

"Malcolm!" I yelled, grabbing at his tail.

He whipped his tail around, shaking off my grip. He then ran from the bathroom and into the hall. I ran after him, but he was too fast.

"Malcolm!"

His strong talons grabbed the floor and propelled him forward. I could see chunks of wood floor flying around like shrapnel. I dove at him, and he grabbed onto the hallway wall and ran sideways for three steps before spinning and diving into the large fifth-floor foyer.

Malcolm turned and faced me. Spreading his red wings, he stood up tall on his hind legs and snorted.

I held up my hands to show that I wasn't going to do anything. I could see the large windows behind him and knew that if he wanted to he could just bust out and I'd never catch him.

"Malcolm," I reasoned. "I'm not going to hurt you. We just need to relocate."

He cocked his head.

"Relocate," I said slowly as if he just needed me to enunciate to clear things up.

I was worried he might go out the windows, but instead he turned and charged directly toward one of the interior walls. He

was so strong he broke right through the wall and into one of
the bedrooms on the floor. Dust and wood flew everywhere as I
stood there in awe.

I could hear him thrashing around in the other room
and then he burst out of another wall and back into the hall.
Apparently he had no concept of doors.

"Malcolm, stop!"

He tore down the hall, running along the floor and the wall.
He would screech and hop back to the other wall to run farther.
He was like a tempest that swirled up and down the walls as he
ran. He reached the end of the hall and turned to look back at
me.

I suddenly couldn't decide if I really wanted him to come to
me or not. The look in his eyes was one of great malice.

"Listen, Malcolm," I said, holding my hands up. "I was just
trying to help. You couldn't stay down there forever."

Malcolm didn't like my discourse. He screeched and came
charging toward me. I moved to the side, and he ran back into
the foyer and through the opposite side wall. Before the dust
had settled, he had come out the other side and was running on
the wall heading in the direction of the bathroom. He skidded
to a stop.

"Hold on!" I ordered him.

Malcolm looked at me and opened his dark red mouth. He

stomped his feet and crashed through another wall into the room right next to the bathroom that was filled with old washers and boilers. He kept going and rammed himself through the inner wall and into the bathroom. As he did, a large iron boiler broke loose from the storage room and crashed into the bathroom. The boiler rolled on its side and stopped in front of the elevator door.

Malcolm jumped over the boiler and climbed into the elevator. He then sat there calmly and looked directly at me.

"Fine," I said. "We'll go back down."

Malcolm snorted.

I squeezed back into the elevator with him and pushed the button. I had no idea it was possible for a dragon to look so smug.

"This is what you want?" I asked as the elevator began to descend. "There's no way out for you guys."

Malcolm didn't seem to care.

"Seriously," I said. "In a day or two you'll be too big to get out."

Malcolm emitted a deep guttural growl. I didn't mean to, but I got goose bumps. I guess there's just something goose-bump-inducing about descending in a secret elevator with a growling dragon.

"I can't keep bringing food down," I tried to reason, barely able to move in the cramped space. "You'll die without food."

Malcolm stayed still.

"Fine," I said again. "I'll keep bringing you food, and we'll figure something out."

The dragon was silent.

"A thank-you would be nice," I said half joking.

I didn't get my thank-you, but when the elevator finally reached the bottom, it was clear that Jude and Paul had been just as upset about Malcolm leaving as he had. All the empty buckets were overturned, and hay was strewn everywhere. The lights I had set up were knocked over, and one of them was smashed to pieces. The generator hadn't been touched, but I could tell by Paul's facial expression that if I had not returned when I had, that too would have been destroyed.

Malcolm joined his companions, and all three screamed in some sort of screechy harmony. It wasn't pretty, but it was nice to see them happy.

"We could all die down here," I pointed out.

They didn't seem to care.

Good things happen to those who work hard. Bad things can happen as well.

The beginning of section twenty of The Grim Knot

CHAPTER 24

What Goes On

EVENTUALLY I GOT BACK UP TO the fifth floor, where I assessed the damage that Malcolm had done. It looked like the entire place was in the midst of extensive and poorly executed remodeling. I knew that if anyone came up here there was no way I wouldn't be busted. My only hope was that nobody ventured past the fourth floor.

I spent the rest of the time that Millie and Thomas were away hauling down more water and supplies. I went to the pantry and took as much food as I could without it being instantly obvious that I had ransacked the place. I took everything that was on the back shelves and the tall shelves. I took things that I knew Millie never used. I gathered a bunch of frozen deer meat that was in the deep freezer in the garage. After all of my hard work, I knew I still had enough food for the next couple of days.

When Millie and Thomas got home, I was sitting at the big worktable in the kitchen, acting as if I were doing my homework.

"Beck," Thomas said.

"Hi," I greeted them. "Back already?"

"It's nice to see you behaving," Millie said kindly.

The three of us had an amazing dinner. Millie made a crusty meat pie with potatoes and gravy that was outrageously good. For dessert we had gingerbread cake smothered in a hot, buttery caramel sauce. Thomas was so taken by the taste that he actually blushed while complimenting Millie.

"Did you see my father?" I asked.

"No," Millie replied. "They're not allowing any visitors."

"For how long?"

"He's not well," Thomas said solemnly, ruining the taste of dessert just a bit. "We are greatly concerned. Although he's had spells in the past, this last year has been a real setback."

My brain pulsated—talking about my father bothered me in ways that I wasn't accustomed to. I felt anger and pity. I also felt fear that he would try and take away what I had. He had tried before and almost killed me. I couldn't let him do it again. I suppose that's why I was so happy to hear he was going to be kept in the hospital.

"Beck," Millie said interrupting my thoughts. "Are you okay?"

"Fine," I said. "I'm just sort of dazed by your cooking."

Millie appreciated that.

"So I picked up your tux for your dance," Thomas announced.

"What?" I asked confused. I had neglected to tell anyone that Kate and I were over and that I wouldn't be going to the prom. I had figured there would be less chance of me having to explain what happened if I never told them it happened in the first place.

"This is so exciting," Millie clapped.

Thomas stepped out of the kitchen and returned with a long cloth bag.

"You shouldn't have," I said uncomfortably.

"It's my responsibility," Thomas said humbly.

"Open it," Millie said with excitement.

I didn't want to open it. I also didn't want them to know about Kate or about how Wyatt was taking her to the prom instead of me.

"Open it," Millie said again.

I reluctantly stood up and hung the top of the bag on a hook on the wall. I untied the bottom of it and pulled the cloth sack up. The color of the tux was somewhere between beige and vomit green.

"Try the jacket on for size," Thomas asked.

"That's okay," I said.

"Beck," Millie snapped. "This is important."

I took the jacket off the hanger and put it on. The lapels were six inches thick and made from heavy velvet. It had gold buttons on the front and a satin trim running down the sleeves.

"My word," Millie said. "You look so handsome."

"Like a true dandy," Thomas said proudly. "Like a dandy. I daresay there will be no other with such finely made formal wear."

That was a dare I wished I didn't have to experience. I hated Thomas's taste in everything.

"Kate's going to go soft in the knees," Millie bragged.

I remembered that I wasn't actually going to the prom. That thought made me feel a little better, knowing that I would never have to wear this.

"The fit is exquisite," Thomas said proudly.

"Now take that off so you don't get it dirty," Millie scolded.

I was more than happy to oblige.

"If you want, we can leave the kitchen so that you can call Kate and tell her what color you're wearing," Millie said excitedly. "She'll need to know for the boutonniere."

I had no idea what a boutonniere was, but the thought of them leaving and me calling Kate seemed like a good one. I knew

I had done a lot of things wrong, but I still believed that if I could just talk to her for a few minutes she would come around.

"Would you like us to leave?" Millie asked.

I nodded, and Thomas and Millie got up and exited the kitchen as if I was a fire they needed to escape from. I waited until I heard their footsteps fade and then walked over to the phone and picked it up. I knew that Kate's parents didn't really like me to call, so I prepared a fake voice and name to give them so that they'd actually hand the phone to Kate.

"Ashley Harrison," I said, practicing to try to sound like a girl.

I dialed Kate's number and waited. After four rings, Kate herself picked up.

"Hi," I said softly.

"What do you want, Beck?"

"I just can't shake the feeling that this might be my fault," I joked.

"I need to go," Kate didn't joke.

"No, wait," I pleaded. "Can't we talk about all of this?"

"I don't trust you," she said. "You've lied to me one too many times, and unless you can explain to me why I should believe you again, there's nothing to talk about."

"Remember how I told you about that problem I had when

I was young?" I asked. "Would someone who wasn't open and honest have shared that?"

"Wetting the bed and destroying the world are two different things," Kate pointed out.

"But they're both kinda awkward."

"I need to go," she said again.

"This isn't fair, Kate," I begged. "You know there are things I have to do."

"Apparently being honest isn't one of them."

"Are you saying that if I had told you, you'd be fine with all this?"

"No," she said, "but I might still care for you."

My heart was not enjoying her tone of voice.

"What about the prom?" I asked.

"What about it?" She was short and cold.

"You're not really going with Wyatt."

"I told you that's none of your business."

"You can't do it," I insisted.

"Really?" Kate said strongly. "I don't think you're in any position to tell me what I can and can't do. Good night."

The phone clicked.

I cleaned off my plate and returned to my room, where I hung up my ugly tux and then spent some time with *The Grim*

Knot. I knew that there were still things inside it that would help me with the dragons below.

After an hour of reading, I stood up and looked in the mirror above my dresser. I looked so different. My dark hair was getting long, and my eyes looked more intense than I remembered them. But the biggest difference was the hardness in my jaw and in my expression. I didn't really like it. I looked like someone I wouldn't want to be friends with.

"That makes sense," I said to myself. "I have no friends at the moment."

I thought about who I had been when I had arrived in Kingsplot and who I was today. The things I had experienced and the stuff I now knew were heavy memories and thoughts. I could see why Kate didn't like me. I wasn't the kind of person that cried, so I didn't. True, there were things that I wish I had done differently, but there was no way I was going to regret planting the last stone. Jude felt like an extension of me, and it was a part of me that I did like.

"Prom," I said aloud. "Who needs it?"

Mr. Binkers just stared at me, gently reminding me that besides Jude, Malcolm, and Paul I had no real friends anymore—and according to most people, dragons didn't even exist.

I lay on my bed feeling lonely and growing increasingly angry.

It took many minds and many ideas to build such a manor. But in the end, ~~everyone~~ some felt it was worth the sacrifice.

CHAPTER 25

Revolution

COPING WITH MY NEW STATE OF mind made the next couple of days horrible. My brain felt like a throbbing bruise that wouldn't stop hurting. I couldn't think straight, and I would get really angry about the littlest things. Wane asked me a question about Kate one night as I was eating, and I could barely contain my rage.

The next afternoon Thomas mentioned that it was going to rain, an event that happens almost every day, and my blood boiled. As I sat eating lunch with Millie on Thursday I felt so out of sorts I wanted to scream.

"Are you all right?" Millie asked me as I ate. "You seem very agitated."

"I'm fine," I said briskly.

"Is it the prom?" Millie asked. "I know how jittery one can become in anticipation."

"It's not the prom," I snapped.

"If you're nervous about dancing, don't worry," she said, scooping a large portion of her sweet-and-sour apple pie on my plate. The smell of the salty sweet apples and butter crust were phenomenal and calmed me down a bit.

"I'm not worried about the prom," I insisted.

I still hadn't told them about Kate and I being kaput, which meant I also hadn't mentioned I wouldn't be going to the prom.

"Just remember," Millie continued. "A true gentleman always leads."

"Yeah," I said sarcastically. "I'm not going to forget that."

"Good," Millie said with satisfaction.

I finished my dessert and went directly to the fifth floor. It was dark, so the destruction and mess Malcolm had made weren't very visible, but I had to be extra careful while walking through it not to trip over anything.

I got to the bathroom, walked around the massive iron boiler Malcolm had knocked over, and grabbed a flashlight. I got inside the elevator and pushed the button. The metal gate dropped.

"Going down," I said with dark satisfaction.

It had been murder trying to keep the dragons fed the last

few days. I had broken into the food storage room where Millie and Thomas had stockpiled things like wheat and dried corn and flour in case we were ever cut off from town for an extended period of time. There were also four cases of sardines and almost a half pallet of chili that Millie had bought from a food wholesaler for a deal. Millie had served the chili once, but it had made Thomas and her so uncomfortably sick that she had stored the hundreds and hundreds of cans away, thinking she would only serve them in an emergency.

It had taken a lot of work, but I had transported most of the food down to the glass cavern. I knew that if Millie decided to check the food stock, I would be discovered as clearly as if someone actually came up to the fifth floor and witnessed the destruction. I just kept telling myself, "A few more days."

I was always thinking that I would soon have a solution figured out, so I had been spending a lot of time down in the cavern opening cans of sardines and chili, feeding them to the gang, and trying to ignore that gnawing feeling in my gut.

The elevator descended.

I could hear myself breathing slowly as the cables squeaked and whined. I felt so attached to the manor. I felt beholden to all its secrets and to the ancestors who had taken the time to feed their manic and oddball desires and wishes by creating a home so perfect for my family and the gift we needed to foster.

I spent two hours down in the cavern. I walked the perimeter with Jude right beside me. I could gauge his temperament and wishes just by looking at him now. Likewise, he seemed to know what I was thinking as I thought it. We were connected, and it felt just as it should.

Malcolm and Paul did their own thing, as usual. Lately they had spent a lot of their time practicing with their wings and screaming. They would open their wings and flap slowly, lifting themselves off the ground a few feet. The ceiling of the cavern wasn't high enough for them to fly freely, so they would just hover and screech.

The dragons were much bigger now. They had grown more rapidly than any of the previous beasts I had raised. Jude was larger than a horse, and the other two were just slightly smaller. I climbed up on Jude's back and looked at our reflection in the glassy surface of the walls.

I looked good.

The ring of uneven bumps around Jude's forehead and right ear had grown into a circular ridge of sharp horns. They looked like a wicked crown. Of course, Jude needed no crown to convince me he was a king. The first dragons I had raised had been very similar to Malcolm and Paul. Lizzy was clearly a queen, but Jude was a king. The connection and communication we shared were far superior to any I had shared with a dragon before. Both he and I knew who he was.

Jude stomped his legs and unfurled his wings. They were long and imposing and made me wish that the two of us were up in the sky flying.

"We've got to get you out of here," I said for the thousandth time.

I think the reason I was so uptight the last few days was because I knew that the dragons would be trapped down here forever unless I figured out what to do. I had taken an ax and tried to bust up bits of the crystal wall, hoping that I would find a hidden tunnel or space behind them, but the walls were solid and my chopping did nothing but break off small shards.

Jude folded his wings, and I slipped off his back. He leaned his long neck down, and I put my arm around his neck, like I was going to give him a noogie.

"I'm glad you're around," I told him. "Everything's crazy, but it seems okay because of you."

Jude tilted his head and looked back at me with his left eye. He snorted twice, and thin streams of smoke rose from his nostrils like gray tentacles. I held onto one of the spikes on his head and shook it softly. His head bobbed from side to side, and he flipped the two ends of his forked tail against the ground. He shifted his weight and nudged me to the left.

"You're by far the coolest dragon I've ever raised," I praised him. "No offense to Malcolm and Paul, of course."

Jude nudged me again, directing me back toward the elevator.

"Fine, I'll be back later," I told him. The words were really unnecessary because he knew what I was thinking.

I got into the elevator and gazed out into the cavern. I looked at the three dragons and pushed the button three times in a tribute to them. The gate dropped and the elevator began to go up.

It traveled about seventy feet and started to slow down. Then it stopped. I looked at the flashlight dangling above me and began to worry about being stuck. Before the worry could grow, the elevator began to rotate slowly. I held onto the sides to steady myself. I could see the wall outside the metal gate moving sideways as the elevator cart turned. It creaked and rotated 180 degrees. Through the metal gate I could now see that there was an opening.

"Wow," I whispered. My heart began to beat at an appropriate rate for someone who had just discovered that the secret elevator he had found had further secrets.

I turned on my flashlight and lifted the metal gate.

"Wow," I said again.

It was a small, finished room. It was no bigger than my

bedroom, but there was a big wooden desk and shelves filled with books. There were cobwebs everywhere, and on the ground was a big dusty rug. I walked around the desk, looking at all of the papers and books on top of it. I ran my finger over one of the papers, and a half inch of dirt came off.

"Wow," I said for a third time.

It was obviously the personal office of one of my grandfathers. There were sketches of dragons hanging on the wall and a small dragon statue in the corner near a globe that looked identical to the one up in the dome room.

A framed large topographical map of the Isle of Man hung on the wall next to the desk, and a spilled bottle of dried black ink lay on the ground.

I sat down in the chair, and dust puffed up and filled the air. I sneezed appropriately. I liked this place. It felt like the lair of an important person. I flipped through the papers on the desk. There was a sketch of the elevator and the glass cavern. I couldn't read all the writing because a lot was faded and the rest was too flowery. Why did people insist on having such fancy penmanship back then? The drawing of the elevator showed the long shaft and the secret room where I now was.

I looked through the books on the shelves and pulled most of them out to check for hidden compartments or anything that might be important. The books looked technical and scientific. Most of them had titles and authors I couldn't even pronounce. There was a small, yellowed folder with the words "The Grim Knot" written across the top of it. I grabbed it and sat back down in the chair. I opened the file and looked at the three sheets of paper in it.

I shined the flashlight at the top sheet.

There were four signatures and a bunch of numbers filling the top third of the page. On the bottom two-thirds were a few lines describing *The Grim Knot*. It talked about its size and color and how all answers were hidden inside. I checked the back of the paper and then shuffled to the next piece of paper. This one was much more interesting. On it was a sketch of the manor that showed all eight floors and the basement. There was a part of the basement that was circled and the letters G. K. were written next to it. On the back of that page was a drawing of the tunnels that led from the basement to the space below the garage where Kate and Wyatt and I had crashed the train.

The third page listed exactly where *The Grim Knot* was hidden in the basement. It revealed the shelf and the book where it had once been tucked away. I figured that Milo had somehow found the room I was now in. He was probably the one who had last looked at this file. There really was no other way he could have dug *The Grim Knot* out of a basement full of dirt without this information.

The only other thing in the folder was a small quote written directly on the back side of the folder that read, "There are answers in beginnings."

"Nice," I said. "There's a news flash."

I closed the folder, feeling like a reporter who had stumbled upon a great lead but was ending up with little more than he began with. I knew *The Grim Knot* held answers, and I didn't need to know where to find it because it was currently up in my room being watched over by a stuffed koala.

I moved the flashlight around the room, looking for anything I might have overlooked. I liked this place a lot. I wondered why the elevator had stopped and turned this time when I was coming up but had never stopped and turned before. I retraced my steps in my mind and thought of anything I might have done differently.

"I pushed the button two extra times," I said aloud.

I flipped through the papers on the desk again and found the elevator shaft drawing. It showed the complete shaft with a row of marks indicating how deep it went. According to the drawing, the glass cavern was almost twenty floors beneath the basement of the manor. The room I was now in was ten floors below.

Next to the cavern was a small number 1. I hadn't thought

anything of it, but I now saw that next to the drawing of the office there was an even smaller number 3.

"That's cool," I said, talking more about myself and how smart I had been to figure it out before I had found it out. "Three pushes."

I searched around for about half an hour more and then got back in the elevator and pushed the button once. It took me straight to the fifth floor.

I washed up and then turned in early. I pulled out *The Grim Knot,* wanting to look at it now that I had read the file. In the past, the book had helped me with a number of things concerning the dragons, but most important it had told me how to eliminate the ones I had grown. I was curious about what Jude, Malcolm, and Paul's weakness was—assuming it would be the same for them all—but I was also scared to know. I figured if I had no idea how to end their lives then I'd never be able to do it and they'd live on forever making the world a better place for me.

"You're so selfish," I told myself.

Sadly, I no longer minded the feeling.

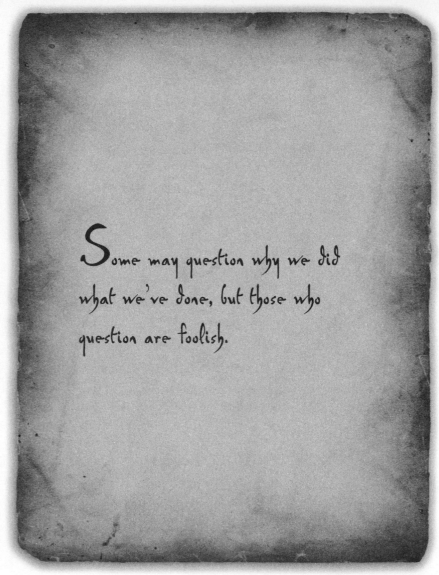

*S*ome may question why we did what we've done, but those who question are foolish.

The beginning of section twenty-two of The Grim Knot

CHAPTER 26

I'm a Loser

KNOWING THAT KATE WAS GOING to the prom with Wyatt was painful. Knowing that today was the day made it even worse. The morning of the prom was cloudy and warm and smelled like summer. I took out the tux from my closet, hoping that looking at it would make me feel better about not going. It was so ugly that it did help a little.

I didn't know what I was going to do. I was anxious about everything. I was worried that someone might go up to the fifth floor and discover the mess. I was worried that someone might go to the food storage room and discover what was missing. I was worried about Jude and Malcolm and Paul being trapped down in the glass cavern forever. I was worried that someone might go to the laundry room and realize that one of the switches on the fifth floor was on. I was worried that Sheriff Pax would show up and arrest me. I was worried that my father was going to try and take what was mine. And I was worried that Kate was going to the prom with Wyatt tonight.

I was a mess.

I was completely on edge. My hands shook, and my eyes seemed to twitch and ache in ways I wasn't accustomed to.

"Kate," I whispered, voicing the worry that concerned me most at the moment.

I'll admit that some tiny part of my brain knew she had every right to go to the prom without me and be happy. That tiny part also knew that it was completely my fault that things had fallen apart and that Kate had dumped me. But, that tiny part was a jerk. The rest of my brain hated that part. The rest of my brain thought that part was weak and stupid.

I just kept thinking of Wyatt taking Kate to prom and how wrong that was. I could see him trying to hold her hand and him saying something stupid and her laughing. They were supposed to be my best friends, but they had betrayed me.

I had stayed up late last night reading *The Grim Knot*. I read about my ancestors living on the Isle of Man. I read about their ability to farm the land and grow remarkable crops that blessed so many. I read about the taxes that forced them to lose so much of their land and wealth. I read about the peddler who had sold them the stones and the resulting perversion of growth and power—the harvesting of dragons and the endless season of pillaging and stealing. I read about those in my family who wished to break the cycle—those who had traveled to America to hide. I read about the building of the manor and the endless desire to once again grow dragons here. I read about my father's father and my dad. I read how the women had gone crazy and how my dad had locked himself up only to succumb to the madness once I arrived here. I read the parts I had added to the book. I then got out a pen and added a bit more. I wrote about the elevator, the glass cavern, and the three dragons that had come from one stone. I described Jude and Malcolm and Paul. I wrote about my father's illness and about my desire to now keep the family's obsession alive.

I had also discovered how the king dragon could be eliminated. I hadn't been trying to, but the answer had come easily to me with some simple information I had found in the folder in the room down below. It made me uncomfortable to have the information. I wanted nothing to do with the extinction of Jude or any other dragons for that matter.

As the day got longer, my thoughts became darker and more painful. At three o'clock Wane came to my room to see how I was doing. I still hadn't told any of them that I wasn't going to the prom. I seriously considered doing so, but I knew it would break Millie's heart. Thomas had offered to drive me and Kate, but I had lied and told him that Kate's mother was insisting on taking us.

"Do you need us to help you get ready?" Wane asked.

"What?" I asked, wearing nothing but my cargo shorts and a white T-shirt.

"Shouldn't you start getting ready?" Wane questioned. "Aren't you two going to dinner first?"

"Probably," I said, caught off guard. I was ready to lie, but I just hadn't figured out the details.

"Probably?" Wane asked surprised.

"Just kidding," I tried to recover. "We are."

"Where?"

"La Fontania?" I said, naming the one fancy restaurant I knew in Kingsplot.

"Oh, that's nice," Wane said. "Do you have reservations?"

I laughed as if I was insulted by her question. "Of course."

"Millie got you a corsage," Wane told me.

I really had no idea what that meant. "Great."

"Thomas said he would shine your shoes, and I can help you with your hair."

What was happening? Suddenly everyone in the manor was obsessed with dressing me up and sending me to the prom.

"This really is an exciting night," Wane said.

"I can tell," I replied.

Wane held her hands out as if expecting a tip. I stared at her until she was uncomfortable enough to explain herself.

"Thomas needs your shoes."

I handed Wane the shoes that Thomas had gotten me. They were already so shiny they reflected light like a mirror.

"What time do you need to be at Kate's?" Wane asked.

"Six?" I said.

"What time's your reservation?"

"Seven?" I said sounding even less sure of my answer.

"Okay," Wane said. "Hop in the shower and then get dressed. I'll do your hair downstairs."

"I can do my own hair," I complained.

"Not tonight," Wane insisted.

"Can I shower alone, or does someone need to bathe me?" I asked.

Wane turned around and left me to shower alone.

I took a shower and changed into jeans and a white T-shirt. I put on clean socks and shoes, wishing I had just told them the truth. When I got downstairs and walked into the kitchen, they all looked disappointed.

"Ahh," Millie complained. "Why aren't you in your tux?"

I actually laughed. None of them laughed back.

"Really?" I asked. "I'm just going to put it on when I get to Kate's house."

"No, you're not," Millie insisted. "This is a special night, and I won't have you showing up in leisure wear. Back to your room at once and put on the tux."

Thomas stood up and handed me two blinding lights. The black patent leather shoes were so polished they looked like small suns.

"Do you need help dressing?" Thomas asked.

This lie was going to kill me.

I stormed out of the kitchen without even answering Thomas. When I got back to my room I threw open my closet door and pulled out the ugly tux. I put the blousy white dress shirt that Thomas had bought me on over my T-shirt. It was tailored at the waist and had humongous shoulder pads. It felt like a superhero Halloween costume. I almost gagged as I was sliding on the pants. The inside was satin, and the outside was paisley-printed velvet.

"Seriously," I said. "Who even makes these?"

The pants had no belt, just a wooden toggle that fed through a loop of material like a latch. There was a zipper, but it was gold and actually made a clicking noise as I closed it. I put on the shoes, tied them, and then slipped on the jacket. I looked in the mirror. For a brief moment I felt like jumping out the window.

"I am so glad I'm not really going," I said to my reflection.

I reluctantly walked downstairs and into the kitchen. Everyone oohhed and aahed as if I were a brand new puppy that could wink. Wane sprayed my hair with some water and combed it into some sort of style.

All three of them then stepped back to take me in.

"My goodness," Millie almost wept. "Don't you look fetching? Just like royalty."

"You are a very handsome young man," Thomas added. "Very handsome indeed."

Wane fussed a bit and then told everyone to step back and give me some air. Millie handed me a flower in a plastic container.

"Thanks," I said, confused.

"It's for Kate," she explained. "She'll have one for you."

"I can't wait."

"Does she know how to pin it on?" Millie asked.

I nodded. I had no idea, but I also had no date, so nobody would have to pin anything on anyone.

"One picture," Thomas said, pulling out a huge camera and wooden tripod from behind one of the kitchen counters. The camera was massive and had an accordion-style lens and a large metal flash.

"No pictures," I insisted, not wanting the moment or outfit to be documented in any way.

"Now, now," Millie insisted. "Just one."

Thomas told me to smile. I didn't. A large flash sparked from the top of the camera, and I could see nothing but a burning white light for a few moments.

"Perfect," Thomas said. "I'll have it developed immediately."

"Can I go now?" I asked, just wanting the entire ruse to be over with.

"Yes," Millie said. "Thomas will take you."

"That's okay," I insisted. "I'll just walk. The roads are dry."

"Absolutely not," Millie said.

I couldn't have Thomas take me; I didn't even have a real date. I was planning just to march down the drive, hike back behind the manor, and then slip through the east door and up to the fifth floor for the elevator.

"I need to walk," I said lamely.

"Why?" Wane asked.

"I'm just so nervous," I said, sounding like an idiot.

They all cooed as if I had just said something really adorable.

"There's no need for nerves," Millie said almost proudly. "Thomas is happy to take you."

"The walk will help me focus," I tried.

"Nonsense," Thomas insisted.

I followed Thomas out to the car with Millie and Wane

waving and cheering me on from behind. I got into the car and shut the door as fast as possible.

Thomas wanted to drop me off right in front of Kate's house, but I talked him into letting me out a quarter of a mile before.

"I just think it will be more romantic if I arrive on foot," I reasoned. "Like a knight."

"Knights rode horses," Thomas said dryly.

"Still," I argued. "Kate's really into people using cars as little as possible. Arriving on foot might score me some points."

"Enough said," Thomas replied with a wink.

I made a personal wish begging the universe to please help me live my life in such a way that I would never again have to witness Thomas winking again. It was the most awkward and creaky wink I had ever seen.

Thomas dropped me off just before the turn in front of Kate's house. I thanked him for the ride; he wished me well and then drove off.

I pretended to march toward Kate's house until I knew that Thomas's car was no longer in sight. I then turned around and headed for home. I could see a car in the distance coming my way. I decided it would be best if I stayed off the road and hiked through the forest. It would take me longer, but nobody would be a witness to my deception or my wardrobe.

I climbed down the side of the road and into the pine trees. I was careful to keep my eyes on all the trees just in case they were in the mood to pick on me again. I heard a twig snap and spun around thinking I'd have to fight a bush or something. Luckily it was just a deer running through the woods.

I hid behind a big tree as the car coming up the road approached. I watched it get closer and then pass by.

"Wyatt," I cursed.

It was Wyatt, driving his dad's expensive car. I wanted to pretend that he was just out for a drive in the mountains, but when I saw the normal tux he was wearing and the direction he was heading, I knew full well that he was going to pick up Kate.

I considered running up the road and confronting the two of them at Kate's house, but when I remembered what I was wearing, I knew the joke would be on me.

I stayed planted at the side of the forest like one of my fellow trees, waiting to witness them coming back this way. Each second I stood there I grew more and more angry. Kate hated Wyatt. She only talked to him because of me. Now she hated me and didn't talk to me because she was too busy going to proms with him.

"I bet she's pinning a flower on him right this second," I seethed.

Finally I heard his car coming back this way. I was standing completely still, but that didn't stop my heart from moving downward into the pit of my stomach. Kate and Wyatt passed by me as if I were nothing more than one of the million other trees in the world. I couldn't tell for sure, but it looked like Kate was smiling.

I bent forward and put my hands on my knees. Something wasn't right. The feelings inside of me were so cloudy and uncomfortable. I had given up everything for something that I couldn't even share with the world. I loved Kate, she was perfect for me. She had been the first person I met in Kingsplot and the first girl I had ever met who made me want to be a better person because of how happy it made her.

Now she had tossed me aside.

I marched with passion through the woods and back to the manor. I didn't know what I wanted to do, but I knew I would think more clearly with Jude around.

When I finally got back home, I sneaked in the east door and made my way up to the elevator room without running into anyone. I stepped into the elevator with purpose and spun around. I was in pain, and the only thing I could think of that would help me feel better was Jude.

I pressed the button just once.

Don't ever forget that the dragons don't really care about you.

The beginning of section twenty-three of The Grim Knot

CHAPTER 27

Blackbird

LOOKING STRAIGHT FORWARD AS the elevator settled, I could see all three dragons waiting for me. They had the appearance of huge deadly dogs that were simply awaiting the return of their master.

That was me.

I threw the metal gate up and walked directly toward Jude. He stood on his back legs and stretched his arms and wings as if I were about to experience one huge hug. He stomped his feet, and I seemed suddenly agitated. I looked into his orange eyes and could tell he saw the anxiety and anger I was feeling.

Jude screamed and snorted, sending sparks from the sides of his closed jaw. Instantly Malcolm and Paul joined in, rocking back and forth while violently flapping their arms.

"Easy," I said, trying to calm them down.

Jude smacked his tail against the glassy soil. The vibration made me tipsy. Malcolm and Paul stopped screaming and took some sort of kneeling position, as if waiting for Jude to instruct them.

I looked at Jude. He stared me down with his orange eyes. I could see his thoughts—emotions he hadn't yet dealt with as a dragon swept through his brain and made me feel for him. I could feel him trying to understand who Kate was and why I was so bothered by her. He opened his mouth and screeched so loud I thought the entire glass cavern was going to shatter on us.

"Hey, Jude," I reprimanded. "Easy!"

Suddenly thoughts of Kate and the danger I could be putting her in by simply thinking about her in the same room as Jude filled my head. I tried to think of other things, but as Jude read my mind the darkness in my own head grew. I tried to think of some dumb song to clear my brain.

"Thomas the tank engine . . . ," I sang.

It wasn't working; my thoughts were still peppered with Kate. Jude screamed again, and Malcolm and Paul extended their claws and dug at the ground. I started thinking of anything cute and calming. I thought of playful kittens I had seen on YouTube and flowers and rainbows, but at the end of each of those thoughts my mind circled back to Kate and the hurt in my heart.

Jude began to come closer to me as if wanting my permission to act out. I knew the dragons couldn't leave the cavern, but I was scared for my own sake. They all flapped around the wood pole in the center of the room. All three of them still felt some pull toward that pole. Jude filled my mind with simple thoughts.

Remove the pole and they'll calm down.

I couldn't tell if it was the voice of reason or not, but they seemed so agitated by the invisible tether the pole created that I decided that if I chopped it down they might settle a bit.

I grabbed the ax and walked up to the pole. I whacked it at the base, and almost instantly they began to settle. I whacked it again, and both Malcolm and Paul lay down on the dirt. I whacked it a third time, and the base of the post split, causing the whole thing to fall to the ground.

Jude sat and stared at me. I couldn't be sure, but I think thoughts of gratitude were filling his head.

"You're welcome," I said. "Now I'm going to go upstairs and change out of this outfit. I'll be back."

A thought filled my head, *What are you going to do about it?*

I could tell the thought was instigated by Jude, and it had nothing to do with my outfit. It scared me to even think about doing something to make sure that Kate and Wyatt understood how mad I was. I couldn't tell anymore where my thoughts ended and Jude's began. I felt justified in my anger like I never had before.

Jude seemed happy with my thoughts.

"No," I said reluctantly, knowing that it would probably be a good idea for me to get upstairs for a bit.

Jude wanted me to stay.

"No," I said again, heading toward the elevator.

All three dragons began to follow me.

"No," I said once more. "I'll be back."

Thoughts of Kate and revenge and getting even and proving my point and putting people in their place and taking the Pillage name where it should go and destroying things filled my head so rapidly I thought I was going to topple. I fought the thoughts and stumbled into the elevator. I pushed the button and turned around. The gate shut, and I could see all three dragons staring at me as if they pitied me.

"Stop it!" I yelled as I ascended. My heart rate felt like a speeding train heading headlong toward the edge of a cliff. I ripped off my jacket as the elevator lifted. I was so hot. My elbows banged the walls as I struggled to take off the shirt. With the shirt and jacket off I felt a little less claustrophobic and could breathe deeply.

"What's happening?" I cried out.

I was rising floor by floor, but I could still hear Jude's chaotic thoughts. I started to pound on the walls of the elevator, begging it to hurry up. It suddenly seemed as if all the air in the world was miles above on the fifth floor. I pulled at the metal gate, pleading with the elevator to move faster. Just as I felt my lungs were going to stretch out and strangle my heart, the elevator began to slow.

I yanked the metal gate up and jumped out. I closed the closet door behind me and walked around the tipped-over boiler. I grabbed one of the window curtains and shoved my face into it to scream.

I felt a little better.

The bathroom was much darker now. The sun had completely disappeared, and shades of gray colored the manor's windows and walls.

"I need help," I said to myself, recognizing that my mind and my decisions were quickly becoming not my own. I thought of my dad and wondered if this was how it had begun for him.

Kate.

I spun around the bathroom as the single word filled me with worry and frustration. I had not thought it.

I needed to lie down. I walked into the hallway, trying to be quiet so that nobody would realize that someone was up here.

As I stepped into the hallway, I heard something behind me

in the bathroom. My head turned around as far as it could. My body then spun to keep my neck from twisting off. I stepped back into the bathroom and grabbed one of the flashlights I had put in the bathtub. I flicked it on and pointed the beam toward the closet door. Everything looked still.

"I'm going mad," I said in all seriousness.

I was about to turn the light off so that it wouldn't appear from the outside as though anyone was on this floor, when the closet door shivered slightly.

My legs did some shivering of their own.

The closet door rattled even more. I reached out and pulled the doorknob to fling the door open. I was prepared to scream, but there was nothing there besides the empty elevator.

Kate.

My mind was frantically trying to tell me something as I watched the elevator box shake. Something was thrusting up from below it. The floor of the elevator began to shatter as Jude's head pushed through like a manic weed bursting through asphalt.

I was scared, but even more, I was thrilled.

Jude ripped the bottom of the elevator with his arms and bit into the door frame with his powerful jaws. Wood cracked and split, spastically tearing the elevator box apart. The seams and structure of the box crumbled as part of it crashed out into the bathroom and other parts fell back down the shaft.

I had never even thought about the possibility of the dragons climbing their way up the shaft. It was much larger than the elevator, and the only obstacle had just been obliterated by Jude. Then Jude threw his arms into the bathroom and pulled himself up out of the shaft. His body cracked the door frame and tore the wall apart. Malcolm and Paul were right behind him. They spilled up from the shaft and into the bathroom like super-sized scaly spiders.

I didn't know whether I should cheer or run, so I decided to just clap excitedly.

Jude looked even larger here in the bathroom. He easily filled half the space. He looked at me, and I knew he was pleased. The weird thing was that I was pleased as well. This was what was supposed to happen.

Jude leaped over the boiler tank and crashed through the far wall. Malcolm and Paul followed after him. There was no way that Thomas and Millie hadn't heard that. I figured we had a couple of minutes at the most before they would be coming up the stairs wondering what was happening.

Jude stopped in the large fifth-floor foyer. He shook his head and then sat like an anxious lion in the middle of the space. Malcolm and Paul seated themselves on either side of him. Jude appeared agitated, like he was fighting to keep still.

"You can't do this," I said, looking toward the stairs and listening for any sign of Thomas or Scott. "I know what you're thinking, and you can't."

Jude stared into my eyes and then, while keeping eye contact, lowered his head to the ground. I knew instantly that he wanted me to get on.

"No," I said sadly.

"*Yes,*" he thought.

Everything I had ever experienced and feared came rushing up to me. I knew that this was the point of no return. If I hopped on Jude's back I would be fulfilling my destiny. If I refused, well . . .

I could hear Thomas and Wane shouting from the floor below. I looked at Jude and wished there was someone here with a clear mind who could bring both of us to our senses.

"Beck!" Thomas yelled. "Are you up there? Are you all right?"

I looked at Jude, and the corners of his scaly mouth seemed to curl. I wasn't all right, but I couldn't let Jude leave on his own because I knew he would find Kate. I had to go with him to make sure she wouldn't be harmed.

Besides, I reasoned to myself—although Jude might have

been giving me his point of view as well—*who can pass up a chance to fly on a dragon?*

I ran toward Jude and jumped onto his neck. I twisted and wrapped my arms around his neck, while digging my feet into his sides behind his wings. Jude lifted his head up and screamed just as Thomas and Wane appeared on the stairs. The last time Thomas had seen me, he had just dropped me off to go to the prom. Now here I was back in the manor on the back of a big black creature. He and Wane looked more than mildly surprised.

I'm not certain, but I think Wane swore.

Jude was obviously not in the mood to be around that sort of language. With me on his back, he turned and ran full speed toward one of the large foyer windows. Thanks to our minds slowly becoming one, nothing he did surprised me. I just held on tight.

Jude leaped through a window as I held tightly to his neck and kept my head down. I could feel pieces of glass flying over me. I could also hear Thomas yelling my name. Malcolm and Paul burst through two other windows so they could keep on our tail.

Jude threw his wings open, and we all shot into the air and down into the Hagen Valley. I could see only one thought flashing through his head.

Kate.

I hoped my mind would stay clear long enough to stop what was about to happen.

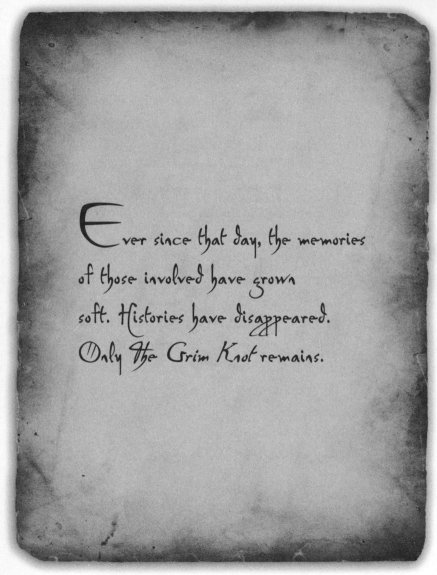

Ever since that day, the memories of those involved have grown soft. Histories have disappeared. Only the Grim Knot remains.

The beginning of section twenty-four of The Grim Knot

CHAPTER 28

I Don't Want to Spoil the Prom

I EXCHANGED THOUGHTS WITH JUDE as we sailed through the sky toward Kingsplot. I kept begging him to turn around and return to the forest. We could hide up in the mountains and possibly never be discovered or caught. Jude wanted none of that; he was on a mission.

Kate.

It was pitch black now, and the town didn't look like much more than a few miles of flickering yellow lights. My dark brain was fighting with me to give in and just enjoy what was about to happen.

"No!" I shouted.

Yes.

My brain kept trying to convince me to go along peacefully. I could hear my own mind whispering to me that I had not brought this upon myself. I had been given the gift, and I had been wrong to suppress any of it. My father and his ancestors had been cowards and fools, afraid to take this gift into modern times, afraid to pillage like we were born to do.

"No!" I shouted.

Yes.

Jude flew swiftly as I held on to his neck, marveling at the ride and trying to think of what I could do to stop what appeared to be inevitable. I looked to my left and could faintly see the silhouette of Malcolm. I looked to my right and there was Paul. I felt connected and part of them. I knew that they had only one purpose, to protect the king. I also knew that as long as they lived, the king was safe. That was great and all, but Jude was on his way to hurt Kate. My own thoughts had betrayed her, and now the dragon was intent on finding her, despite my constant yelling and demanding that he turn around.

We dropped lower, and I could see the spires of two churches and the top of the Wiggendale Museum. Jude slipped even lower and flew just feet above the ground over a field of clover. He knew where he was going because I knew where he should go. Directions didn't matter when you shared so many thoughts.

"You can't do this!" I yelled. "Kate helped raise the others. She raised the queen."

I couldn't stop my brain from remembering, however, that she had also helped kill the queen.

Jude screeched and blew fire directly in front of him. The flame pushed back and wrapped over his head, down his neck, and past me. I was suddenly warm and then cold again.

"Please stop!"

I could feel Jude's clear drive to finish what he had set out to do. He wouldn't let me think him out of it.

Jude twisted to the east and headed straight for Callowbrow. Prom would be in full force by now, and Jude was in the mood to cause some havoc. He flew over the assembly hall at Callowbrow and then lifted higher to circle the building. Malcolm and Paul drew in closer, flying mere feet behind us. I could see cars pulling up to the front of the hall, and people in beautiful dresses and normal-looking tuxes getting out and walking in.

There was a red carpet and a huge banner in front of the door with the prom theme, "On the Wings of Love," printed on it.

I could hear music thumping in the hall. It was muffled, but the sound filled the air beneath us. I saw Wyatt pull up to the school and help Kate out of the car. They were far away, but even from this distance she was beautiful. She had on a pink dress with short sleeves, and her hair was arranged on top of her head with a few strands dangling down in front of her eyes.

Kate.

Jude turned his head to lock his gaze on her. We both watched Kate and Wyatt walk down the red carpet and into the assembly hall. Jude tilted and turned sharply to circle over once more. Malcolm and Paul mimicked his moves completely.

There was no way that this could end well. I needed Jude to forget Kate and help me get him to safety before it was too late. I kept trying to distract his thoughts with other thoughts, but it wasn't working

Kate.

Jude tucked his wings and dove straight for the roof.

"Stop!" I ordered, but he wouldn't hear of it.

He reached his legs down and grabbed hold of the huge air-conditioning unit on top of the roof. Without a pause, he flapped his wings and yanked the unit off its footings and into the air. It was too heavy for him to carry much higher, so he let go, and the entire unit rolled along the roof and tumbled down into the grass on the side of the building. Jude flew back up into the sky.

"What was that for?" I yelled, wondering if he was simply going after metal objects like his predecessors had.

As Jude twisted and turned to circle back, I could see that the spot where the air-conditioning unit had been was now occupied by Malcolm and Paul, who were tearing at the roof with maniacal abandonment. It didn't look like anyone below had realized what was happening yet.

"Don't do this, Jude," I pleaded.

Jude twisted again and tucked his wings. He shot toward the front doors of the assembly hall.

"Nooooooo!"

I held onto his neck as tightly as I could, knowing that I might not live much longer. Jude flew directly into the large glass front, smashing through the doors with his thick skull. I was hanging on for dear life as he righted himself and stomped into the lobby. Everyone began to scream and scatter. I used the fear of the moment to roll off Jude and onto the floor. I couldn't let him find Kate and hurt her.

Jude crashed through the interior doors and into the large open hall. The music kept playing even though everyone was running for their lives. I could see bits of the ceiling falling from above as Malcolm and Paul broke through the roof and made their own grand entrance. I ran in behind Jude, quickly scanning the fleeing crowd for any sign of Kate and Wyatt.

Jude bit one of the massive speakers and then picked it up with his mouth and flung it across the hall. The speaker shattered as it hit against the wall.

Kate.

My heart couldn't take much more. I felt so helpless and more than just a little responsible for what was happening.

I looked over at Jude and saw him spot what he was looking

for. I traced his gaze and could see Kate at the edge of the room standing still as everyone else ran past her. She looked horrified, but not surprised by these events. Wyatt was begging her to run to safety, but she wouldn't budge.

Jude stomped closer toward her.

I pushed through fleeing students, hollering Jude's name and then Kate's over and over. Malcolm and Paul were flying and jumping around the hall like madmen. They were biting at everything and swatting tables and chairs everywhere.

Jude reached Kate and stopped ten feet in front of her. Kate just stood there, mesmerized by the beast. I wasn't completely surprised by her reaction. Kate and I had been through a lot with dragons, and she had always been rather taken with the beasts. In fact she had enjoyed their company even more than I had. Sure, she had lost interest as soon as they had turned on us and tried to destroy us, but until that point she had been a team player.

Jude faced Kate and opened his mouth.

"Noooo!" I shouted as I jumped in front of Kate, acting as if I were a secret service man who was willing to take a bullet for her. There was no bullet, and no bite for that matter—I crashed to the ground, landing on my right shoulder. Both Kate and Jude stared down at me.

It wasn't my proudest moment.

I scrambled back on my feet and stood in front of Kate and

Wyatt while facing Jude. I held my arms straight out from my sides as if to protect them. Jude just shook his head and snorted over and over. We were encircled with scared and escaping students, but it kind of looked like Kate and Wyatt and I were all preparing to dance the spotlight dance with the dragon.

"That's him?" Kate asked in awe.

"Yep," I replied as students and faculty continued to dash from the room screaming.

"There are two others," Kate observed.

"Yeah," I replied while breathing heavily. "The one stone hatched three."

"I'm sorry I took Kate out," Wyatt whimpered, thinking that I had brought the dragons to teach him a lesson. "I just came to meet girls."

"Thanks," Kate said sarcastically.

"What?" Wyatt replied defensively. "Everyone knows you love Beck."

I wanted to stick around and really discuss that, but I needed to get Kate to safety and get Jude away from all these students. My head was filling with Jude's confused thoughts. I grabbed Kate's hand and pulled her away from the center of the hall and toward the stage at the east end. Wyatt followed us with Jude right behind him. The crowd of students and faculty had cleared off the floor and there was nobody except a few people still hiding behind tipped-over tables and torn-up bits of ceiling.

"Get to the stage!" I yelled.

We hopped up on the stage as Malcolm and Paul swooped in screaming from behind Jude. Kate, Wyatt, and I crouched behind the stage curtains, pretending that we would be safe there. Through a crack in the curtains I could see two security guards rush up to Jude from behind. They both had Tasers and shot them toward Jude's rear end.

It was a really stupid idea.

The Tasers didn't even faze Jude, but they angered his guardians. Malcolm and Paul spun and blew fire toward the now-fleeing guards. The flames melted the bottom of one of the guard's shoes as he ran. Fire slipped up over the floor of the gym and lit two tables on fire.

"What are you doing here?" Kate said urgently.

"I came to save you," I yelled, watching Paul tear a wall apart. "It's not going so well."

"We have to get them out of here!" Kate said, finally willing to help me.

"I knew you'd come around," I said back.

"You ruined prom," Kate snapped as we cowered behind the curtain.

"It'll still be a memory," I pointed out. "Just a really terrifying one."

Jude reached out with his right arm and swiped at the curtain. It ripped and fell to the ground in one big heap of red velvet. Kate, Wyatt, and I were exposed like a bad magic trick.

I stood up and put my palms out. Jude kept his gaze locked firmly on Kate. I could tell by his thoughts that he wasn't clear about what he should do. All the anger I had felt toward Kate was getting mushed up with the feelings of concern I had for her.

"What now?" Wyatt asked.

"This is why I told you not to plant that stone," Kate argued.

"I was trying to help my father," I argued back. "I couldn't let him just suffer."

"Didn't he try to kill you?" Wyatt asked.

My thoughts raced toward my feelings of my father. He had tried to kill me once. He had tricked me into planting the last stone. He had used me before and tried to use me again in the hospital. I loved him, but he had never been well enough to care for me.

Jude disengaged from the staring contest he was having with Kate and looked at me.

He was pulling at my thoughts and thinking of my father.

I watched the dragon's mind switch gears. It was clear that

I cared for Kate, but it was also obvious I had father issues. I didn't necessarily want him going after my dad, but it seemed like the only way to get him and Paul and Malcolm away from the school.

My father is the problem, I thought.

Jude seemed almost happy with the new direction. Malcolm and Paul stopped tearing at the door the security guards had run through and flew over to stand on either side of Jude. Jude lowered his head, and I turned back and looked at Kate.

"Do you want to stay here?" I asked. "Or come with?"

"Hey," Wyatt protested. "She's on a date with me."

"Come on," I waved.

As I turned back to Jude, he read my mind perfectly and screeched. Malcolm and Paul lowered their heads. I hopped on Jude, while Kate got on Malcolm and Wyatt leaped on Paul. I wanted to give some sort of command to make it look like I was in charge, but before I could say a word, all three dragons shot off from the stage and up through the hole they had created in the roof.

I breathed a small sigh of relief, knowing that for the moment Kate wasn't the target, she was part of the team.

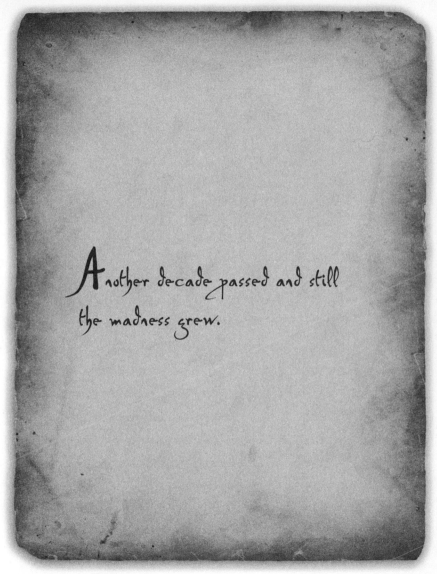

Another decade passed and still the madness grew.

The beginning of section twenty-five of The Grim Knot

CHAPTER 29

I'll Cry Instead

VERY STEALTHLIKE, WE FLEW through the sky as if we were jets, just without all the noise and pollution. The only sound was that of flapping wings and Wyatt occasionally screaming like a little girl. The dragons swooped and rocked in smooth, easy motions as they piloted their way over Kingsplot and toward the hospital my father was locked in.

I could see the large, lit, glass atrium that rose from the middle of the hospital like Matterhorn Mountain at Disneyland. I had wanted to save Kate and get the dragons away from Callowbrow, but now I was afraid I was heading into something equally harmful. My dad was not well, and I wasn't sure if him being attacked by dragons was the best thing for his condition. I tried to reason with Jude as we flew, but he had such a one-track mind. He had read the hurt and betrayal I felt, and I knew that until he finished this objective he wouldn't easily move on to the next.

"We could go through the front door!" I yelled to Jude. "If we ring the bell they might just bring him to us!"

Jude wasn't buying it. He wasn't the kind of dragon that stopped to ring bells. He much preferred bringing down the roof. I squeezed his neck, tightly pushing the side of my face into his skin. Jude blew out fire, and the puff of warmth rippled over me.

Malcolm and Kate flew up behind Jude, and Paul and Wyatt maneuvered to a position to their left. Then, like three darts on the same trajectory and traveling at the same speed, all three dragons with us onboard shot directly toward the glass mountain in the center of the hospital's roof. I closed my eyes. It was the third glass structure I would be flying through tonight. And even though Jude's head always seemed to absorb the blow well, it was still not an easy feeling flying directly into glass.

Jude hit first, crashing through the glass roof and down into the small plants and trees that were growing around the indoor atrium. Metal brackets and glass rained down in a massive tinkling fashion.

Malcolm and Paul came in right behind us, screeching as they arrived.

Alarms sounded immediately, and lights flashed on as orderlies seemed to come out of the woodwork. Instantly there were dozens of beefy men in scrubs. They looked at the dragons and had a quick change of heart. All of them turned and started running away. I had no idea where my father was, but I knew that the lady with the big nose was in charge.

I only had to think it, and Jude reacted.

He ran toward a set of locked double doors and charged through them like a multihorned cosmic bull. The doors flew open and off their hinges. Malcolm passed us running on the wall. Kate was holding onto him as tightly as I was holding onto Jude. I tried to think of something else to get Jude's mind off the poor woman in charge, but it was hard to think of something I wanted Jude to harm instead.

I kept thinking of produce and bad weather, seeing how I would have no problem with Jude taking on broccoli and a rainstorm, but it didn't work. Jude stomped down the hall toward the front. The woman with the big nose was cowering behind the desk, frantically trying to call someone for help. Jude opened his massive jaw and screamed. Spit flew everywhere, covering the walls with wet, dark patterns. The black dragon stretched his neck over the desk and looked down at the woman.

She didn't sound very professional when she screamed.

I looked beside me. Kate and Wyatt were still on their dragons, holding on for dear life. Three huge orderlies came running at Jude with some sort of metal sticks. Before they could get anywhere near him, Paul and Malcolm moved into their path and knocked them to the ground. I could see Wyatt and Kate desperately trying to hang on during the scuffle.

I turned my attention to the woman behind the counter. "Hello," I yelled.

Jude pulled back a bit, and the woman poked her head up just enough to see me.

"I need to talk to my father, Aeron."

"He's not here," she whimpered. "Is that a . . . ?"

"Have you never seen a dragon before?" I asked incredulously. "Well, now you have. So where's my father? You guys had him locked up."

"Dragons aren't real," she said, crying.

All three dragons screamed in an effort to help her see reality.

"Sheriff Pax has him," she said shaking. "He came yesterday and ordered his release."

"That's impossible," I said again. "Why would . . . ?"

I shouldn't have thought it, but the thought went something like this: Sheriff Pax had gotten my father out of the hospital so that he could take him to the manor, use the elevator, and find the dragons that belonged to me. My dad didn't care about me; he cared only about the dragons.

It was just a quick thought, but it was enough to change

Jude's focus again. He spun around and roared. I tried to thank the lady for the information, but Jude was moving so quickly that I'm not sure she heard me.

Malcolm and Paul got in line behind Jude as he ran back down the hall knocking out ceiling tiles with his head and wings and breaking anything that wasn't as wide as him. I could hear Kate and Wyatt yelling things, but I couldn't understand them due to all the tearing and ripping of building materials.

Jude slammed through the same doors he had busted moments before and then leaped upward. He flew out of the shattered atrium and straight up into the night sky. He flapped his wings and quickly shot east.

I was fighting my brain, trying to get my thoughts to stay clear. I was scared to think about anything. I knew I was simply postponing the inevitable by not thinking, but someone was going to get seriously hurt unless I got Jude under control.

"Calm down!" I ordered.

I could feel him resist and reject those thoughts. Jude wasn't in the mood for anyone to control him. He was beginning to recognize his position and with each new moment his thoughts became stronger and less of mine and more of his. He could feel the division between me and my father. He also understood that whereas I wanted nothing more than to protect him, my father wanted to take him away.

It was very cold as we flew over Lake Mend and the old ball bearing factory. And it was even colder as we traveled into the mountains toward the manor. Jude kept blowing fire, and the warm flames washed over us like small blasts from a furnace. I couldn't tell if he was doing it to keep us warm or because he just wanted to show off.

"Don't kill anyone," I kept saying aloud, hoping the message would sink in. "Don't kill anyone!"

The dragons in the past had gone from pets to pillagers quickly and once they had turned, they no longer had any affection or concern for me or anyone else. Jude was different. We both understood that we needed each other for this to continue, for his species to carry on.

"Still!" I yelled. "Don't kill anyone!"

I could feel his thoughts, and they were focused only on finding my father in the cavern.

One of the best things about traveling by dragon is the speed. We didn't have to drive slowly up the steep, winding road. We simply had to soar straight up the mountainside and into the forest above Kingsplot. It took us a few minutes to do what it usually took an hour to do in a car.

I could see the Pillage manor. Not a single light was on. Every floor was dark. Even the lights lining the driveway were off.

Jude circled the manor and then swooped into the same

fifth-story window he had broken out of. He settled in the foyer as Malcolm and Paul entered behind him. I looked over at Kate. Her hair had blown free of the pins holding it in place, but she looked wonderful, although a little ticked off. Wyatt was holding onto Paul's neck so tightly that the poor dragon began to choke and shake. Wyatt let go and slipped off the dragon like a fried egg out of a Teflon pan. I climbed off Jude and ran to Kate. When I reached out to help her, she refused to take my hand.

Apparently she was still holding a grudge. I tried not to think poorly of her for fear of Jude reacting to it.

It was dark in the manor, but our eyes adjusted. Kate's once-beautiful dress was torn and blackened all over. It was obvious that Malcolm had blown a little fire in flight as well. Wyatt stood up. He didn't look right in a tux. In fact, it looked more absurd to see him dressed up that way than to see him standing next to a dragon.

The last time I had been in this room, Thomas and Wane were there. Now it was completely silent. There was destruction everywhere, and I could see through the giant holes in all the walls. It made the fifth floor feel much more open.

"What now?" Wyatt asked.

I couldn't answer Wyatt yet because I was focusing on singing another song in my head to keep my thoughts from thinking anything that might prompt Jude to leave or kill someone. I kept singing the theme song to *iCarly* over and over.

Jude looked mad about my taste in music.

"Are you humming something?" Kate asked.

Jude turned and began to run toward the bathroom. Malcolm and Paul surprised no one by following suit.

"Go downstairs!" I yelled at Wyatt and Kate. "Find Thomas and Wane."

"Okay," Wyatt said.

"No way," Kate disagreed.

"You don't understand," I pleaded. "I don't know what's going to happen."

"That's your best attribute," Kate said. "I'm not going downstairs."

Apparently Wyatt didn't appreciate that part of my personality. He took off for the stairs while Kate followed me into the bathroom. The whole fifth floor was so torn up that there were no doors or completely intact structures anywhere.

"Those dragons can't fit in the elevator," Kate commented as we ran, showing she had a pretty good grasp of spatial relations.

"There's no elevator anymore," I said, jumping over a big chunk of hallway wall. "They climbed up the shaft."

"That shaft has to be half a mile long," Kate said, baffled.

"They're dragons," I reminded her.

When we got to the bathroom, I could barely see the tail end of Paul slipping down into the shaft.

"Is your father down there?" Kate asked.

"I can't imagine how he would have gone down," I said, "but he's with Sheriff Pax."

The closet where the elevator used to be was nothing but a huge, torn-apart hole. There was no door frame, and almost all the wall was ripped out from between the two windows. The large iron boiler was still lying sideways on the floor a few feet away from the shaft, making the place look like a war zone.

"What happens when they get down there and find nothing?" Kate asked.

"They'll probably climb back up and demand I think of something."

"So what are you thinking?" she asked.

"I don't know," I said defensively. "But I'm not killing them."

"Do you know how?" Kate asked, knowing that for every dragon it was different.

I told Kate how I had figured out that by putting the first letter of each chapter of *The Grim Knot* together it had spelled out the answer. "They have to be killed with the same single blow."

"How do you do that?" she asked.

"It doesn't matter," I said firmly. "I'm not going to kill

them. I'll run away. I'll hide them in the forest for the rest of my life if I have to."

"This is why I broke up with you," she said. "You're going to end up like your dad."

"And what's wrong with that?" a dark, new voice asked.

Kate and I spun to the left to see where the voice had come from. There in the corner of the bathroom was my father.

It scared me so badly that I fell backward against the iron boiler. I stood back up as quickly as I could. Kate grabbed my hand, and I could feel her shivering.

"Dad," I said quietly, wishing I could see better in the dark.

"'Dad,'" he mocked. "I don't know who you're talking about."

The honesty in his voice scared me more than his surprise. It sounded like he completely believed he wasn't my father.

"We've been waiting," he whispered.

"We?" I questioned tentatively as I reached into the bathtub and pulled out one of the two remaining flashlights. I flicked it on. On my short list of wishes, near the top would be that I wished I had never done that.

Kate and I were suddenly surrounded by hundreds of plants. Ivy was stretching in through the windows and hung from the roof, bushes snarled in the corners, and long, willowy ferns covered the walls like a jungle. As scary as the plants were, what they were doing made them that much worse. This may sound like a medicine-induced dream, but all of them were wielding weapons. Some were jabbing forks and sticks while most had small kitchen knives and blades in their palms and leaves. I saw one plant shift a sharp knife from one of its branches to another as if preparing to slash me. It looked like my father and half the forest had been waiting in ambush.

My father smiled and I could tell by the crazy glint of his eyes that his mind was completely under the influence of darkness.

"The dragons are mine," he said sternly.

Kate slipped behind me.

"No way," I argued. "I raised them, and they know my mind."

"Your death will change that," my father insisted.

"You're forgetting something very important," I said, trying to remain calm.

"What's that?" my father humored me.

"These plants respond to my wishes also," I said boldly. "I can just as easily turn them on you."

My father let out a deep, guttural laugh.

"What's so funny?" I asked as the plants stretched their limbs and shook.

"They might listen to you on occasion," he said, "but it is my word that controls them completely. Like the king dragon who listens first to you, the soil always takes my side. Who do you think has been controlling them all this time?"

"Wait," I whispered. "The plant that attacked me at the hospital months ago?"

"I needed you to be motivated to plant that stone."

"The mushrooms?"

"I needed that stone as well."

"The cactus?"

"Fear is a great motivator."

"What about the tree ambush?"

"I wanted the dragons to myself," he whispered sinisterly.

"I'm your son," I said sadly, feeling the sickness of our blood swirling and boiling beneath my skin.

"I don't know what you're talking about," my father said for the second time.

Kate and I tried to back up, but plants began to fill the space behind us.

I was beginning to fear for my life, which just so happened to be the perfect thing to do. I could feel Jude down below in the glass cavern with Malcolm and Paul. I could feel him sense the danger I was in, and I could feel him begin the long scramble back up the shaft.

"Don't be too disappointed," my father said. "The sickness would have killed you soon anyway. I'm just speeding things along. Pillages have never had the strength to think beyond themselves."

Kate held my hand as we backed away from my father. I looked at her, and she looked at me. I saw the fear and sadness in her eyes. I also saw an idea forming in her mind. It was as if I could see inside her head.

The idea was impossible.

She glanced at me and nodded slightly. Her body was trembling with fear, but her shoulders were squared. She looked like she had been through one heck of a prom. She had the answer in her head, but I couldn't do it.

Kate squeezed my hand.

My mind was pushing out, trying to make my head explode. I'm not sure why, but I started to cry and sob. My shoulders shook, and I knew what I had to do.

I could feel Jude as he climbed up the shaft recognize what I was thinking. There was a sudden crippling panic in my chest.

"What's the matter?" my father barked.

Kate squeezed my hand one last time, and I knew there would be no other opportunity. With a like mind we turned and took two steps, slamming into the iron boiler. It was extremely heavy, but it rolled toward the large hole where the closet door used to be. I could feel Jude screaming and clawing up the tunnel with Malcolm and Paul behind him. His shock at my betrayal made me sob harder.

"Stop!" my father yelled. "Attack!" he screamed, ordering every living thing to tear into Kate and me.

It was too late; the heavy iron boiler gathered enough momentum to roll over the floor edge and into the shaft. Strings of ivy pulled Kate and me back as the boiler dropped down the shaft, heading straight for Jude. My brain screamed, and I begged Jude to forgive me.

We could hear the boiler crash madly down into the shaft.

I fell to the floor crying as plants sliced me up. The pain they were inflicting wasn't half as horrible as the searing hurt in my head. Jude was screaming, and his fear felt like a hot poker against my naked eye.

"You fool!" my father screamed, diving toward me. Just as he fell on top of me, an earth-shattering explosion shook the entire manor. I rolled across the floor and into Kate, and we turned to see a fireball of flame burst up out of the shaft. The boiler had not only crushed the dragons, but it had set off an explosion that must have blown the glass cavern to smithereens.

My father seethed and lay still on the floor as the plants in the room withered and retreated. Kate was leaning up against the tub, looking like she hadn't really enjoyed her prom like she thought she would. I slid down and leaned into her. I then cried until every ounce of water in my body was used up.

The king was dead.

Don't trust anyone.

The beginning of section twenty-six of The Grim Knot

CHAPTER 30

Let It Be

EVERYTHING HURT FOR A LITTLE while. I'd really love to say that from that moment on it was all great, and, of course, I'd also like to say that I'm better than Kobe at basketball. Some things just aren't true, and the truth is, it took me weeks to smile again—I just felt so awful about what I had had to do.

Thankfully, after a few weeks, things cleared up inside my head, and I began to feel happier than I ever had. It seemed the boiler had not only killed the king, it had destroyed all the darkness in my head.

After the explosion, my dad was rushed back to the hospital where he remained in a coma for three days before he woke up crying. I was there when he woke up and did a little more crying of my own. I'm not really a big fan of guys weeping, but we both finally realized that even though the dragons were gone, we were going to be all right. It also kind of felt like we were finally meeting each other for the first time.

My father would have never been at the manor that night if not for Sheriff Pax. The sheriff had been so consumed with figuring out his own memory loss and how to protect Kingsplot that he had foolishly taken my father from the hospital. My dad had promised Sheriff Pax that all the answers he sought were in the manor. But when they arrived at the manor, my dad had been a less-than-perfect host, ungraciously thwacking Sheriff Pax on the back of the head with a shovel. He had then forced Scott to tie the sheriff, Thomas, Wane, and Millie up in the kitchen.

Scott reluctantly had done so.

Scott had actually been reluctantly doing things for my father for some time now. Unbeknownst to any of us, Scott and my father had been communicating in secret. It was Scott who had turned the water on in the bathroom and let the sink overflow. Scott had been my dad's mole. Unfortunately for Scott, being a mole didn't stop my dad from hitting him with the shovel after he had tied up the others.

After my father had everyone tied up, he had climbed to the fifth floor. There he had discovered that the elevator was temporarily out of order. So my dad had decided to wait in the dark and use the element of surprise to finish me off and claim the dragons for himself.

As you know, it didn't quite work out like he had planned.

The explosion had done way more damage than I had anticipated. It had not only killed the dragons, but it had obliterated the elevator shaft and cracked part of the manor's foundation. I had thought the weighty iron boiler would crush the dragons in the shaft, but I had never anticipated the boom. Sheriff Pax informed me that many of those ancient boilers were like bombs due to gases that had built up in them over the years and their lack of use. I was also pretty sure that the gasoline I had stored for the generator probably contributed to the big bang as well. When Kate heard I had stored gas down there she was amazed, and not in a good way. Apparently that was a bad idea seeing as dragons breathe fire. I had never thought of that, which Kate pointed out was one of the reasons I wasn't fit to be a dragon raiser. She was probably right, but it didn't matter anyway. There would be no more dragons to raise in my future.

Sheriff Pax was very kind to me and our family as we all tried to sort out what had happened and what should take place next. He knew that in time the memories of what had happened would fade, so he was always writing stuff down. He could have locked up my father or me or caused all kinds of problems for us, but in the end his only concern was this:

"Get those old boilers out of your home," he had said. "I'll get some of my men to do a check for you. We've got to keep you safe. I couldn't bear to see something else happen to that manor."

I told him he gave adults a good name, and he told me that he would never forget I had said that. I also promised him that he had more than made up for killing that turtle years ago.

A marvelous thing was occurring in Kingsplot. It seemed as if the fog had lifted. The morning after the explosion the world was a sunny place. The clouds kept to the highest mountains, providing rain and keeping the rivers alive, while making it possible for the valley to finally get a light tan. Green like I had never seen filled the fields, and trees that used to huddle and shiver now stood tall and welcomed the days.

Kate and I had survived a lot—angry dragons, knife-wielding plants, and an explosion. Plus, I had ruined her prom and lied to her repeatedly. She had every right to still be angry with me, but she wasn't. I guess the fact that I had read her mind at the right time, and then acted on it, seemed to erase almost all of her bad feelings for me. She knew how hard it was for me to destroy Jude and Malcolm and Paul, and apparently she felt as if I had suffered enough. Compassionate and beautiful—she was pretty much perfect.

Wyatt was the most put out of everyone. He had been in the

kitchen untying people when the explosion had gone off. He had missed the action in the manor, but more important, his prom had been ruined, and that prom had been his chance to, as he put it, show the ladies what he had going on. I figured I had done the entire student population of Callowbrow a favor by putting a stop to that.

Since the death of Jude, not a single plant had bothered me. I had a feeling they never would again. It was hard for me to come to terms with the thought that I would not see another string of ivy growing under my command, or ride another dragon, but a clear mind and a sane father seemed like a pretty fair trade.

My dad was released after just two more weeks in the hospital. He was a different person. In fact, he didn't even look the same anymore. His hair was short, and his face was clean-shaven. He seemed twenty years younger and at least two inches taller. The weirdest thing was that he was always smiling.

I could finally see the resemblance.

He now also had a personality and presence that drew people near instead of driving them away.

Wane and I drove down from the hill and picked my dad up. The lady with the big nose was waiting with my father in front of the hospital when we arrived. I hopped out, and I walked to my dad. I was taller than him now, and we still had a bit of catching up to do, but we were going to be just fine.

Big Nose saw my father to the car and then waved good-bye as if she really cared.

"Wane's driving?" my dad said as he and I climbed into the back.

"Not if you'd like to," Wane offered.

"No," my dad laughed. "I'm fine, I just thought Beck might want to."

I looked at my dad and tried to figure out who he was. Since the moment I had arrived in Kingsplot I had been begging him to let me get my license.

"I don't have a driver's license," I reminded him.

"We need to fix that."

My dad seemed way smarter now.

Wane drove along the old highway and toward the mountains and around the lake. The day was warm, and fat flocks of fowl flew in clusters over Lake Mend.

"This is a historic day, Beck," my father said happily. "Just think, two Pillage men returning home healthy."

I couldn't help but smile.

"I feel so light," he said.

"Maybe you should put your seat belt on then," I suggested.

My dad put on his seat belt and looked at me.

"Beck, you have saved me," my dad said seriously, as Wane tried hard to pretend that she wasn't listening in.

"Ah," I waved. "It's just a seat belt."

"Not that," my father said with emotion. "It was a fortunate day when you came to Kingsplot. Look where we now are."

"Well, it did get a little messy between then and now," I reminded him. "Not everything's gone smoothly."

"I heard about the prom," he said sympathetically.

"Really?" I asked. "With all that's happened, that's the detail that sticks out?"

"I know Kate wanted to go," he explained.

"Wow," I laughed. "You've obviously been talking to Millie."

My dad laughed and changed the subject.

"I can't wait to see the manor," he said with excitement. "There's nothing like clear thought. I feel like my life has just begun."

I wanted to point out that despite all the changes he had made, he was still kinda old. Instead I said, "Yeah, the manor's an incredible place."

"I wonder," he said reflectively.

"What?" I asked as the car began to climb upward on the winding road.

"There's something I think we should do."

I listened carefully to my father's idea.

CHAPTER 31

The End

SUMMER WAS LIKE A DREAM, and warmth filled the Hagen Valley in buckets. Gone were the gloom and misty grayness that kept everything so closed in and wet. Kingsplot was alive with sounds of life and celebration and progress. There was even talk of the public library getting Wi-Fi soon. Tonight, however, the real celebration was taking place miles above Kingsplot. You see, despite all the happiness in my life at the moment, I still felt a little bad. I mean, sure, I had saved my family, but I had ruined Calloway's prom. My father's idea had been to throw a formal party at the manor to make up for it.

Yeah, my father.

I saw the wisdom in his idea instantly. So with a lot of

planning and some help from everyone, I put together a little formal bash at the house, and tonight was the night.

The house of Pillage had never looked more amazing. Millie, Thomas, Wane, and Scott had gone all out. They had hired dozens of temporary helpers for the house and gardens. There were candles in every window and lining the drive. It looked like the Milky Way had settled right here on earth.

The first floor had been staged and set up with decorations, and tables and chairs ensconced in material. Everywhere I looked I could see candles in odd shapes and sizes, their wicks winking with light and movement. The manor was so clean and decorated, I hardly recognized the place.

I hired a deejay who promised he would play only things we approved of, and I begged Millie to dazzle us with her food. I had never seen such a small, old person jump so high. It was as if her entire life had been a buildup to that one request. Thanks to her, the manor now smelled of amazing food. I knew there wouldn't be a single guest who would go home hungry tonight.

My father and I knew the party wouldn't make up for everything we had done to Kingsplot. It wouldn't even make up for me destroying the Callowbrow assembly hall and ruining prom, but I wanted it to feel like we were at least trying. Wyatt suggested we use the old prom theme, but I had never really liked that cheesy theme. So, Kate and I came up with a new, much less romantic one:

Themes Are for Books

Wyatt painted the theme on a big banner and hung it beneath the three gargoyles perched atop the driveway gate.

At first I was worried that nobody would make the drive up to the manor, but by the time the party was in full swing, there were hundreds of couples there. Everyone came wearing the tuxes and dresses they hadn't gotten the chance to show off properly at the prom.

I had changed as a person, but I still wasn't humble enough to wear what Thomas had picked out. So I had driven myself with my new license into town and rented a regular tux. Now as I stood in the foyer of the manor and welcomed people, I looked at myself in the entryway mirror. The black-and-white contrast of my outfit reminded me of the prison jumpsuit I had once worn.

I kept checking to see if Kate had arrived. I knew her dress had been destroyed by dragons, and I was curious what her new one would look like.

Principal Wales and his surprisingly attractive wife came in through the front door. Invitations had been sent out to the entire Callowbrow faculty as well as the students. I was surprised how many faculty members had actually shown up.

"This is a noble gesture," Principal Wales said as he entered the manor. "I've longed to see the inside of this beautiful home."

Wane and Thomas took their coats and motioned for them to move into the main hall and see a bit more.

I glanced around, wondering where Kate was.

Professor Squall came in with the curator from the museum. I shook their hands.

"Again," I said. "Sorry about that display and all."

"Water under the bridge," Mr. M said, handing his coat to Wane.

Not only was it water under the bridge, but Mr. M had given me a gift. While they were putting the display back together they couldn't figure out which Pillage the bronze statue was. Not even my father knew. So, the museum had given it to us, and we put it up near the end of the driveway as a reminder of all our ancestors and the amazing things they had been through to help bring us to this moment.

Students continued to pour into the manor. Kids who had always rubbed me wrong were now all smiles and kind words. I thanked everyone for coming, but I was still waiting for the most important guest.

I looked around at the manor and marveled at how beautiful things were. I didn't know for sure, but I had a feeling that someday my memories would be fuzzy and that certain things would be forgotten. I smiled knowing that at least I had *The Grim Knot*. It had helped in so many ways, and I figured it would help in the future to keep my mind filled with all that had happened.

My dad came up next to me.

"You doing okay?" he asked kindly.

"Yes," I answered, knowing I wouldn't be doing great until Kate arrived.

People just kept coming and coming. The driveway and road were lined with hundreds of cars now. As the crowds coming in began to decrease, I started to worry about whether I had said something to make Kate stay away.

I looked past the foyer and into the main hall where the music was playing and people were dancing. I could see Wyatt happily dancing with a girl he had liked for years but had never had the courage to talk to. I guess formal parties just bring out the best in people.

Of course, the best person still was a no-show.

I was about to walk out and go search for Kate when she finally walked in. I looked at her across the room and realized that she was way too good for me. She didn't have on a dress;

instead she was wearing her faded Beatles shirt and blue jeans. She had her hair back, and her blue eyes were drawing me in like magnetic oases.

I walked across the foyer, suddenly feeling way too over-dressed.

"What are you doing?" I asked her.

"I couldn't find a dress I liked," she replied, smiling.

"You look amazing," I told her.

"You too," she said looking at my tux.

"What?" I asked defensively. "The invitations *we* sent out said formal, remember?"

"I know," she said apologetically. "I just started thinking about all the people who would be here and having to sit down and talk to everyone."

"I love how antisocial you are," I complimented her.

"Hey, Beck," she said softly. "Remember that false floor you found in that room on the fourth floor last week?"

I nodded.

"Did you ever check it out?"

"No," I said. "I usually do that kinda stuff with you."

Kate smiled, and my fingers and toes popped. She had a strange, wonderful effect on me.

"Well," she hinted. "There's no time like the present."

I leaned in and kissed Kate. I kissed her because I loved her and because she was my girlfriend and because she was beautiful, but mainly I kissed her because she had her priorities in order. I pulled back and looked into her eyes.

"Let's go see where it goes," she whispered.

"I love you," I whispered back.

The two of us made our way to the fourth floor as half of Kingsplot ate, drank, and made merry in the name of Pillage.